Cabin of Memories

and Other Short Stories

Misan Akuya

Published by Revival Waves of Glory Books & Publishing

PO Box 596| Litchfield, Illinois 62056 USA

www.revivalwavesofgloryministries.com

Revival Waves of Glory Books & Publishing is committed to excellence in the publishing industry.

Published in the United States of America

Paperback: 978-1-365-87408-6

Contents

Night Time Is The Right Time

"Here's your coffee." Said the waitress. I had ordered a regular coffee, black with some sugar packets.

"Thank you." I said as she walked away. It must have been 12 noon or something. Perhaps a bit too late for coffee. But coffee has never worked too well for me anyway. It wears off pretty quick. I just like the taste. It's always better when someone is at the other end of the table though.

Then I looked up and saw a woman. She was reading a book. She looked like someone that had been haunting my dreams. But in a good way. She had raven black hair. Short. But not too short that it appeared that she was attempting to make some sort of statement. She looked like a type of chick that took no bull from anyone. But kind at the same time. She wore no makeup. But unlike some other women, this did not hinder. Perhaps it aided her, it exposed her natural beauty.

I all of a sudden had all of these feelings arise in me. It was as if this woman was activating memories that I had long forgotten. Without even speaking to her I was having an emotional response. I knew that I had to speak to her.

I got up and walked right to her. I submerged all of my feelings of nervousness as I walked over to her. I knew that I had to meet her.

I arrived and she looked up to me. Her eyes were greenish brown. And they had a sparkle to them. She looked mystical without trying. Most women could only achieve that by wearing some sort of garden crown on their head.

"Hey." I said to her. "I don't believe that I've ever seen you here before."

"Doesn't look like it." She said with this ooze of coolness.

"Let's rectify this." I said. So far I was on point. I sat down right in front of her. She appeared impressed by my take charge attitude.

"Name's James." I said.

"Katrina." She said as she took a sip of her drink. I believe that it was some sort of tea. Perhaps green tea.

"Is this your first time here?" I asked.

"At this hour." She replied. I had a long night.

"Ah, what happened?" I asked.

"Let's just say that I am not having any dinner tonight." She said.

"We'll that sucks." I now were are just going to have to get drinks." I said with such confidence that I had a cool experience happen to me. I can't say that it was an out of body experience. I was firmly in my body. But it was an out of mind experience. I was so impressed with myself. She just smiled realizing the good game that I was spitting.

"You're so cute." She said.

"I wish someone would just say that "you're so hot." I replied.

"Depending on how you are you could be a bedroom nine." She said. I could tell that I was getting her on my hook.

"What are you reading?" I asked with honest curiosity. She picked up the book and showed me. It was Infinite Jest by David Foster Wallace.

"Oh wow, good luck" I told her.

"I got through in search of lost time, I'm good". I said with a smirk.

"I love Proust." I said. She began to light up.

"He knew what he was talking about." She said.

"At least he did at the end." I said.

"What do you think that he was trying to tell us? " She asked as though she hadn't come up with a concrete conclusion of her own.

"I believe that he was saying that art gives life meaning." I said." That it allows us to escape the dread of our everyday life.

"That's my guess." She began to smile. I believe she was liking what she was hearing.

"Look, I got to go." She said which made me believe that what I was doing wasn't working.

"But, we should hang out tonight." Whew.

"Yeah, sounds epic." I said regretting using the word epic. It was not epic. It was cool. Epic made it sound like I barely got women or something.

"Yeah, epic." She said with a devilish smile. "Why not spectacular?"

"Let's see your performance first." I said. I couldn't believe what was leaving my mouth. I was still on a bit of a roll.

"Good point." She said. She took my hand and wrote her number on it. "Call me." She said as she got up and walked away. Even the way that she walked was cool. She had such grace at style. Yet didn't feel airy.

I sat there just staring at my hand. It had worked. I got initiative. I went for what I wanted. And I got the result that I was looking for. I now had a hot date.

It was night. I had texted Katrina and the date was all set up. We were to meet at time square, get some drinks and see a show. After which I had a game plan to get her back to my place a good time. Everything was in place and I couldn't wait.

I began walking down towards time square. I had a little pep in step. I love how this place looks at night. I always imagined that the electricity used here could power a small country with ease. But hey, it's America so, reasons.

As I continued to walk a woman ran into me. She was pretty. But she looked a little off. She was dressed up a bit sloppy. None of her clothes fit. Her hair was nice and messed up at the same time. I didn't want to jump to conclusions. But I was pretty sure that she was a hooker.

"Are you okay?" I asked with genuine concern.

"Yeah, I think so." She replied.

"Great, I've got to go." I said as I started to walk off. She then grabbed my arm.

"What?"

"Want to hang out?" She asked in a desperate way. I surveyed her and it was confirmed that she was a hooker.

"What's your name?" I asked.

"Abigail." She said.

"James." I replied. "Look, Abigail, you seem like a nice girl..."

"Thank you." She said.

"But I have other plans, I have to go." I told her as her heart sunk.

"Come on!" She exclaimed as she went off as like a child. "Don't you want to have some fun?"

"I already have something going on." I told her.

"Nothing like me." She said as she showed some kind. I was a little impressed.

Then all of a sudden this man runs up towards us. He was wearing a bandanna, a gold tooth, and he was wearing a purple leather jacket. He was clearly a pimp. Yay.

"What in the hell are you doing?" The pimp asked Abigail commandingly.

"What's it to ya?" Abigail replied with confidence that was beginning to come out of nowhere.

"I own you." He said as he turned to me. "Do you have anything to do with this?"

"Nah man, chill." I said suddenly attempting to talk street.

"Don't play with me cuzzo." The pimp said as he drew a knife on me.

"Look, I don't want any trouble." I told the pimp. "I was just on my way."

"Is this true?" The pimp said as he turned to Abigail. Abigail then got this smile and twinkle in her eye indicating to me that she was about to lie.

"He was trying to get it in for free." Abigail told the pimp smiling at me the whole time."

"You have got to be jacked up!" The pimp yelled as he swung at me. I was able to duck and run. The pimp started chasing after me. I began running as if I was running track.

I ran for a good for blocks until I made a turn. I then ran into this woman big time. I knocked her on to the ground. She looked like Winona Ryder from Beetle Juice. She had the Gothic get up and everything.

"I'm sorry!" I said. "Are you okay?" I extended my hand to help her up. As she got up a fake spider fell out of her purse.

"Yeah, I'm fine now." She said with this beautiful creepy smile. I don't know why, but it seemed like I was all of a sudden hot stuff. Like the smell of me going on a dating was attracting women towards me. Only weirdos.

"Glad to hear it." I said as I began to think of my way out. "I'll see you around."

"Wait!" I said. "I'm Callie." She said.

"James." I replied.

"James." Callie said as she got in closer to me. "We just had a meet cue." I held back rolling my eyes.

"Excuse me?" I said.

"A meet cue." She said. "It's a beautiful thing. "It's in the movies. "When two characters meet together for the first time in an interesting way. "This was it."

"That sounds nice." I said going for the easy letdown. "But I really have to go."

"You don't like me?" She said with these pup eyes.

"No, no, no." I said. "It's just that I have other plans, I have to go."

"Come on!" She said giving me some deja vu. "Keep it loose!" She then went into her purse and handed me a piece of hair.

"What is this?" I asked with curiosity.

"It's a merkin." She said as I jumped back. The chick officially crossed over to crazy person territory.

"Look, I'm going." I said still trying to be nice.

"What is your problem?" She said.

"I have no problem." I told her as I began to make my exit.

"You're weird." She said. "Creep."

"What?" I asked with confusion.

"Creep!" She yelled. "I need help!" She continued to yell.

I suddenly saw three guys start to come towards me. I was in a position again where I had to run. And I took off. This world was relentless. I could hear her in the background going "he's going that way!

"Don't let him get away!" I suddenly had three guys, I believe Hispanic, chasing after me.

I continued to run into I got back into the middle of time square. I was able to loose them after a while. I was drenched with sweat and smelly as hell. I saw a store, went in and sprayed myself with old spice. I was ready for the date.

Somehow I wasn't more than five minutes late. I ended up not too far from the location. My luck appeared to have been getting better. I couldn't believe it.

I started walking down and I saw her. She looked fantastic. She was wearing this black little dress with red leather boots. Without makeup, she looked gorgeous. With makeup, she was other worldly. I was beginning to get excited again. This was a hot date. And despite all of the events that have taken place tonight, I was ready.

I walked to her and said her name. She turned, gave me a glowing smile and a big hug. The hug was one of the warmest hugs that I had ever had. And after how the night had gone, I really needed it.

"Hey!" She said with a smile. "Great to see you!"

"Great to see you too." I said with a slight sigh of relief. "You wouldn't believe what's happened to me."

"What's going on?" She asked.

"Don't worry about it." I said as I began to guide her as we walked away.

The night appeared to have finally turned a corner. It looked like everything I went through was maybe for a reason. Now I would get to relax and be on a date with this great girl.

"What do you think of strap ons?" She asked with honest curiosity. This, of course, caught me off guard and I needed a beat to gather myself back up.

"Come again?" I asked hoping that I just heard wrong.

"What do you think of strap ons? She asked again. It appears that my strange night was not over.

"As in using them?" I asked.

"Well, them being used on you." She said with honest eyes.

"I'm not into that." I told her bluntly.

"You don't like to experiment a little bit?" She said with a twinkle in her eyes. I could see where this was going.

"Do you use strap ons a lot?" I asked her.

"I tend to gravitate towards them for sure." She said. I couldn't believe what I was hearing.

"How many guys have you used it on?" I asked her almost not wanting to know the answer.

"Not just guys, girls too." She said with a smirk. While the girl part soften the blow a bit, it was clear that this chick was a freak.

"Well, it's not my thing." I reiterated.

"Lighten up, trying some things." She said as she slapped my ass and decided to put her finger in it. I jumped up like a horse.

"What are you doing?!?" I exclaimed. "I never want anything going in back there!"

"Just a compliance test." She said as if she was making complete sense.

"Who are you?" I bluntly questioned her with 100% seriousness. This was not what I had expected.

"I'm just a girl that into things." She said with a great deal of innocence. Yup, she was crazy. A bit bat crazy if you asked me.

"If I were up for anything what would you do to me?" I asked regretfully. Part of me just wanted to see where this would go.

"I'd tie you up, ball bust you, slap you around, get the strap on and then have it." She said with a glowing smile to my horror.

"What has happened to you?" I asked with fear.

"The same thing that happened to that chick from 50 shades of Grey." She told me.

"Look, I don't know how this is going to work on." I told her.

"Quit being a baby." She said as she poked my ass again. This time I had enough.

"Stop!" I told her. "What is wrong with you?" "I just wanted a normal date with a cool girl and it looks like I stumbled upon the craziest femdom bdsm fanatic out there!"

"So you know what's good?" She replied.

"Goodbye." I said as I walked away.

"Come on!" She yelled. "Once you get it on your back you can never go back!

I walked away with a great deal of anger. I couldn't believe how the night had turned out. Nothing had gone right. All three of these women that I meet tonight were attractive, that's for sure. But all three were messed up in their own unique way. Whatever happened to meeting a normal girl? Getting drinks and seeing a show? Does that still exist?

As I got back on the main streets I looked across the street and of course I saw Callie, Abigail, and the pimp. They had a nice crowd of other guys with them too.

"There he is!" Callie yelled. "Get him!"

They began running after me like the crazy mob that they were. I smiled for a quick second and ran off. It looked like my night was just starting.

Cabin of Memories

Saturday, 10:30 am. Trevor was laying down on the couch. Dr. Leykis was sitting down listening to him. Trevor has had a lot of problems lately. These problems have driven him to go and get a shrink. A shrink that demanded $200 an hour.

"Life isn't just what I thought it was." Trevor told Dr. Leykis.

Dr. Leykis appeared that he was aggressively taking notes. But he was working on a drawing that he felt was just the bees knees. He was a robot. He wasn't sure what kind of robot that he wanted to draw.

"I knew it wouldn't be easy." Trevor continued. "But I didn't think that life would be like this."

"What did you think it would be?" Dr. Leykis asked taking a break from the action.

"I don't know." Trevor pondered. "More fun?"

"What is your definition of fun?? Dr. Leykis asked actually getting interested.

"It was hanging out with my girlfriend." Trevor said with a heavy heart.

Trevor's girlfriend, Sara, was no longer with us. She has passed away. Leukemia was the perpetrator. She was only

23 years old. It didn't seem fair that someone so young would die of cancer. Her parents had to watch her die. Going to her funeral was a nightmare for Trevor. He just about did not want to go. But he knew that he had to. And it haunted him.

"I just haven't been the same doc." Trevor managed to muster out. "I just can't get passed this."

"Son, you need a vacation." Dr. Leykis said pretty much grabbing something out of his ass. "You need to get out there and do something."

"Like what?" Trevor asked hoping for some magical answer.

"Like camping." Dr. Leykis said to Trevor's dismayed. Trevor hadn't been camping since middle school.

"Why camping doc?" Trevor asked.

"You need a break from everyday life." Dr. Leykis said now actually engaged. "You need to go and clear your thoughts." Right now everything that you do is clouded in the past. You need to be able to break free from this."

"And roughing it will do the trick?" Trevor asked not really buying it.

"Get a cabin, I don't care." Dr. Leykis said probably annoyed that he had to pay attention to Trevor. "Just go out there and clear your mind.

And that was that. Trevor decided to take the dr's advice. He came to the conclusion that he had nothing to lose. He couldn't do anything without thinking of Sara. If he looked at the sidewalk a certain way he would think of Sara. He would turn on the shower and think of Sara. He would eat Captain Crunch and think of Sara. He could not get away from her. And it was stalling out his life.

Trevor worked as a cashier at Bullseye. But he hasn't been able to focus on his job in a while. When a guest would annoy him, Trevor would give it right back to them. That was a big no no at Bullseye. He's had to speak to managers about that on several occasions. When he wasn't doing that he was just disengaged. He wasn't interested at all in his job. Not that he was in love with it to begin with. But he used to be able to find something fun about it. Now he lives in dread every day at work.

So he figured that this trip could do him some good. He began to develop a fuck it mentality when it came to this trip. So fuck it why not?

Before he left he went to Danielle's apartment. Danielle was Sara's best friend. The two had become particularly close since Sara's death. They have both even developed romantic feelings for each other. But of course neither one of them knows that they like each other. And neither one of them feels comfortable with disclosing this kind of information to each other. It just didn't seem right in this context.

"You're doing what?" Danielle asked with disbelief.

"Camping." Trevor said. "The dr thinks that I need to do it."

"Have you ever even been camping?" Danielle asked with even more disbelief. It seemed like she just couldn't see him camping.

"Yeah, like in middle school." Trevor said beginning to become a bit annoyed with Danielle's vocal tone.

"Sorry." She said. "You just don't strike me as the camping kind."

"Well, I'll be roughing it for the weekend." Trevor said confidently.

"Look at you." Danielle said trying to make Trevor feel good. "A regular Davy Crocket.

"Please." Trevor said. "Daniel Bloom."

And so Trevor was on his way. He packed his bags, got himself a nice raccoon hat, got in his car and was off. There was this nervous energy in him. It was as if he felt the rumblings of something crazy about to happen. But he just could not put his finger on it. That feeling of knowing something was just around the corner. But not being able to describe it.

He drove down this somewhat weary road. It was only somewhat weary because of how it looked. It had this Tim Burton aesthetic to it. Kind of quirky, but off enough it was a little scary. It felt as though if he said Beetlejuice three time that the demon was going to just jump out of nowhere.

As Trevor arrived the vibe went from Tim Burton it Sam Raimi. The feeling as though some fucked up shit was about to take place. And you better hide. Oh, you better hide.

Despite all of this Trevor decided to step lively and go in. The cabin was a lot better on the inside. A bit dark and creeky. But not as bad as he thought it would be. Then all of a sudden he saw a shadow that wasn't his own. He knew it. He was in the real life Evil Dead. Only he was on his own.

"Welcome." An ominous voice said.

"Who the hell are you?' Trevor asked just hoping it wasn't some crazed serial killer."

"I'm going to be your guide." The ominous voice said.

"Show yourself." Trevor said just about scared shitless.

The ominous voice appeared. He was a tall bald man. He was dressed in all black. If he wore sunglasses he would have looked like someone from the matrix. He didn't smile though.

"Better?" He asked.

"Better." Trevor said.

"Okay. Let's get down to business." he said making Trevor all the more confused.

"What is this all about?" Trevor asked.

"You are in a cabin of memories." The man said.

"A Cabin of memories?" What in the hell is that?" Trevor asked feeling as though he was starting to lose his mind.

"This cabin has all of your memories." He said as though he was trying to freak Trevor out. "Every wall hear is filled with your memories.

"But how is this even possible?" Trevor asked.

"Thing of this cabin as if it were a parasite." The man explained. "You are now the host." So now this cabin has now absorbed all of your memories."

Trevor couldn't believe what he was hearing. He was really beginning to regret listening to his shrink. Now he was in a less than favorable situation. He was standing in front a random man who was telling him that the cabin that he was in is, in fact, a parasite. This would creep anyone out.

"So what does all of this mean?" Trevor asked just trying to piece all of this together.

"What any of this means is completely up to you." The man told him. "You decide what to do with all of this."

"What should I do?" Trevor asked just trying to get some help.

"I cannot tell you this." The man explained. "You must figure it out."

"What is going to happen?" Trevor asked just seeking bread crumbs.

"You will be revisiting memories that pop up the most in your mind." The man said.

"Why?' Trevor asked.

"Because that is what you want." The man said.

All of a sudden the man disappeared in a flash. And Trevor was left alone. This creepy feeling came over Trevor. This feeling of being trapped. He had felt that he had been trapped in his mind. But now he was trapped in a cabin that was filled with his mind. And this was not a pleasant though.

Trevor began to make himself a sandwich trying to forget what had taken place. It was a nice Ruben sandwich. He ate with that feeling of you trying to ignore a feeling that is within you. But a part of you just won't allow you to do so. A part of you was crying out to pay attention. But he persisted and continue to eat the Ruben.

Then all of a sudden a bring light came in a flash. He was transported to the library. He was looking for books. Then Sara was appeared. This was the first they had met. And he had been transported there. She had her Burnett hair, quirky glasses, nice skirt, and red shoes just how he remembered her. He could smell the library. It had this fancy professional smell with a hint of lavender. It was just like how he remembered it.

Sara started walking towards him. He wanted to do something. But he realized that he couldn't move. He couldn't do anything. He was just along for the ride. He could only watch his memory take place.

"Do you need help?" Sara asked. She was a librarian.

"It depends on what kind of help." Trevor said. He remembered his lame attempts at pick up lines.

"Help as far as finding the book that you are looking for." Sara explained.

"Ah, yes." Trevor said trying to think of what next to say. "I didn't realize that librarians like you were allowed."

"What do you mean by that?" Sara asked with suspicion.

"I'm just saying that I don't recall seeing the cute librarian." Trevor said licking his chops.

Sara began to blush. As Trevor watched this from the stratosphere he couldn't believe it. It was as if he was watching a movie of his life starring him. It was one thing to think of the memories. But to see them right in front of him was a whole kind of psychedelic experience.

Suddenly Trevor was sucked back into reality. He found himself sitting down once again. He got up and walked around. He checked out his hand. He couldn't believe what just happened. He didn't know if had just had a dream, or if that was the real deal. He needed answers.

"Yo! "What was that?!" Trevor cried out.

The man appeared as flashy and ominously as he did before. But this time, he was actually smiling. He knew that Trevor had experienced something. And that the night has merely just begun.

"How was it?" The man asked trying to hold back.

"What the fuck was that?" Trevor asked clearly shaken up. "How did that happen."

"You didn't enjoy the memory?" The man asked.

"That's not the point." Trevor explained. "I came here to get away from those memories. "Not to experience them again."

"Think of it like going to the movies." The man started. "You are merely watching some movies here. "Really short films."

"I'm not in the mood for that movie." Trevor said. "Can't you make it stop?"

"That power lies within you." The man explained.

"What?" Stop that shit." Trevor commanded grasping at straws.

"Only you can "stop that shit." The man continued. "You have to find the will and the power to do so."

"How do I do that?" Trevor asked.

"You already know." The man said.

Just as Trevor was going to ask another question the man vanished like that. Trevor was once again alone. He was starting to feel so disorientated. He didn't know what to make of this situation. How could he just enjoy it? Seeing Sara's face so clearly was too much for him to take. He just wanted to get away from her. He needed to get away from her.

And just like that he sucked back in. This time, he was at the beach. He knew exactly where he was. He and Sara were walking hand and hand on the boardwalk walk. It was a nice and sunny day with a nice breeze. The ocean looked as green as ever. You could hear someone playing the ukulele in the background.

"I like going to this beach." Sara said glowing.

"Yeah, just wish the water wasn't do green." Trevor said in a funny, yet downer way.

"Just don't eat the fish in it and you are good." Sara said.

"I am not so sure that swimming in it is such a good idea either." Trevor said.

"Ba!" Sara balked. "Don't let lame shit like that stop you."

"Lame shit that get me a disease." Trevor said. Trevor was starting to remember how much of a downer he could be.

Sara then grabbed his arm and ran off with him. She was taking him right to the water against Trevor's will. She wasn't truly strong enough to over perform him. He was letting her drag him. Part of him loved what she brought out him. How she made him feel like he was alive. He never got this feeling from anyone else.

Once they got in the water she began splashing him. He wasn't really down with this at first. But he warmed up to this. They began to splash each other back and forth. Suddenly Trevor felt free in the water. He didn't care that the water was green. As Trevor watched this he watched with the feeling of tears developing. He could vividly see what made Sara so special.

And then he was sucked back to reality. This time, he was more disappointed. He was actually enjoying that. He realizes how much of a downer he has become lately since Sara's death. Even before her death, he was a downer. But she evened him out. But without her, he had no enthusiasm for life what so ever. So he knew what he had to do. He had to kill himself.

He picked his cell phone to call Danielle. He was going to tell her how he felt. Figuring that he would be dead that it wouldn't matter if she felt the same way. Even if she did he couldn't go on like this anymore.

"Hello?" Danielle said.

"Danielle." Trevor said.

"Hey, what's up?" Danielle asked. "How's the camping?'

"Look, I need to tell you something." Trevor said.

"What's up?" Danielle asked with concern.

"I am going to end it tonight." Trevor forced out. "And I just wanted to say that I love you."

There was silence on the phone waves. Danielle was trying to process what she was hearing. She couldn't believe what was happening.

"Trevor..." Danielle started.

"It's okay." Trevor said as he interrupted her. "I've got to go."

"But Trevor, I love you too." Danielle said stopping Trevor in his tracks.

"I'll see you again someday." Trevor said as he dropped the phone.

And that was that. He was ready. He began to walk outside to contemplate on how he was going to end his life. He didn't just want to cut himself. He didn't have a gun. But then he remembered the cliff near by. He would just jump off. It would be quick and easy.

As he walked to the cliff he was yet again sucked into another memory. This time, it was in his own bath tub. He and Sara were together. Watching this memory was hard to bare for Trevor. It was one of his most treasured memories.

He watched as he cleaned her and she cleaned him. How she splashed him, he splashed her back, and she softly slapped him over the face. Then she came over and caressed her. She was so warm and bubbly.

"I wish that we could just freeze this moment in time." Trevor said with the biggest Mickey Mouse smile on his face.

"I wish that you would come up with better lines." Danielle said smiling at Trevor.

They began to splash water at each other again. And the splashing turned into passionate kissing.

Trevor was then sucked back into reality. And had become a reality that he just couldn't live with anyone. It only furthered his decision to go ahead be done with his life. He just couldn't go on living like this.

Trevor started to run towards the edge of the cliff. He ran as fast as he could run. He ran faster than Forest Gump. He just put his blinders on a ran.

He stopped himself just as he got to the edge of the cliff. He looked down. Then he looked up at the sky. Perhaps remembering the lyrics from the Metallica song for whom the bells toll. He took a deep breath and jumped.

As Trevor jumped one more memory came into his head. He was sucked back to it in mid air. He and Sara were sitting on a couch. She had the ukulele.

"Sing something." Trevor said looking lovingly at Sara.

"Like what?" Tara asked.

"Anything." Trevor said. "I know that you'll make it sound pretty."

"Okey dokey." Sara said in the cutest way.

She began to play this song. And it was one of the nicest songs that anyone could have heard. Every note sounded perfect. It was charming in every single way.

Then something happened. Trevor wasn't quite sucked out of the memory. But he could see himself falling and the memory at the same time. It was this incredible bittersweet feeling that was occurring. As the song completed Trevor hit the ground and died instantly on impact.

A week later there was a funeral. It was tough on everyone. Particularly Danielle having to watch two of her best friends die. She was filled with tears the whole time. She couldn't believe what had just happened.

As she left the funeral a black car stopped right in front of her. When the window was wound down it was the man from the cabin. But, of course, she didn't know it.

"Hello." The man said.

"Hello." Danielle said trying not to cry.

"I am not sure what happened, but I am sorry for your loss." The man said. "I think that I can help you."

He handed Danielle a business card. Danielle inspected this business card. The business card was cool and slick. It simply said THE MAN.

"Thank you." Danielle.

"Don't be afraid to reach out." The man said.

"I won't." Danielle replied.

"Will be seeing you soon." The man said as he drove off.

And little did she know that this was just the beginning.

Santa Monica

It was a nice Saturday night at the Fairmount hotel in Santa Monica. This was perhaps the nicest hotel in Downtown Santa Monica. Usually reserved for the richest out of towners and their yuppie kids.

But it was the yuppie in Towner kids that had a room in it tonight. Clint and his girlfriend Maria were throwing a dinner party. Or should it be said that Maria was throwing a dinner party and Clint was just along for the ride?

Maria loved any opportunity to make herself look good. Living in Los Angeles felt like a full-time job to her. She did all that she could do to keep up with appearances. She made a good living. But she was nowhere near one of the richest girls out there. So nice dinner party in a nice hotel would give a greater impression of wealth then there actually was.

How did they afford such an expensive room?

"I love credit cards." Maria said with a vapid smile. Clint was sitting down watching TV annoyed.

"And the debt collectors love you." Clint replied to Maria whose face turned into a frown.

"Clint!" Maria barked. Clint turned around his head. She stared at him expecting him to stand up. He eventually did.

"Clint, this is an important night as I have informed you, you do understand this?"

"Yes." Clint said trying to not viscountess roll his eyes.

"So, I need you to be on your best behavior tonight, got it?" Maria asked as if Clint was her five year old son.

"You got it, dude." Clint said stealing a line from Full House.

"That's all I am asking." Maria said sounding appeased.

"And you'll get it." Clint replied.

"I've been looking forward to this night for so long you won't believe it." Maria said. You could tell from her overall presence that she had been perhaps waiting for this moment way too long. Like she had nothing better to do for too long.

"I'm sure it will live up to your expectations." Clint said to further appease her.

She then walked away. The door bell rang. As Clint went up to get it he started to really dread the situation that he found himself in. He didn't want to have to be a part of some fake dinner party. He didn't want any part of this madness what so ever. He just wanted to have dinner and drink. Preferably without Maria. Maria was just starting to get on his nerves. He couldn't even remember what it was about her that drew him to her anymore.

He opened the door and it was Robert, the butler. He was a black British butler like Jefferey from Fresh Prince. He was proper and you could tell that he's been doing it a long time with the nice brief case.

"Is this the dinner party?" Robert asked.

"Unfortunately, you have arrived." Clint said bummed out.

"Excellent, you sound very excited." Robert said wondering what was with the attitude.

"Sorry, I am still just trying to wrap my head around this." Clint responded trying to save face.

"It's fine." Robert told him conveying that he understood. "I know that it's not for you."

Clint let Robert in just as Maria walked into the living room. Maria's face lit up like it was Christmas day and she had finally gotten that easy bake oven that she had always wanted. Having a British butler at her dinner party was perhaps just as good.

"Robert!" Maria said as she ran up to him and gave him a hug. "Now we can really make this special."

"I'll do what I can Maria." Robert said like Clint trying to not roll his eyes.

"Let me take you the dinner room." Maria said. "I think you'll be impressed with what you have to work with."

Maria then guided Robert to the dinning room. Clint was already getting tired of the night. He didn't want to be apart of this at all. But he had no options. It was as though Maria had him by the balls. Part of him wanted to just runaway and never see her again. But that wasn't going to go down. That just was not going to happen. He was stuck there and he would have smile even though he was worried.

So he did the only thing he could do. He took out his bowl, packed, went out to the balcony and smoked it.

Smoking weed was the only thing that really calmed Clint down. Drinking helps too. But for Clint, he preferred smoking weed for cognitive reasons. He was able to get himself on to another planet. He was able to get himself far, far away from this place. Somewhere that Maria wasn't.

It wasn't that he hated Maria. They had been together for two years now. It was that he was tired of her. They met doing a play together. And then her mother died. This put her into a vulnerable situation and Clint felt bad for her. They had sex the night of the funeral. They have been together ever since. Their relationship was built on sadness.

Now Maria has been used to using Clint as an emotional tampon since. He really helped her get over her mother's death. And ever since then she thought that this was Clint's role in the relationship. And Clint did for a while too. But that while didn't last forever. Clint now could see what Maria was doing. And was sick of it. He didn't want her to bleed her emotional problems on to him anymore.

Each inhale and exhale was like being able to be apart of something new. He hated L.A. But being able to smoke weed so freely was undeniably one of the benefits of living in L.A. No one cared that you smoked weed. Most people did. If a cop confiscated your weed they would more than likely just smoke it with a bong that they confiscated too.

The doorbell rang once again to Clint's dread.

"Clint!" Can you get it the door?!" Maria commanded.

Clint dragged himself in. He was pretty high at this point. But he had gotten so high so many times that he could handle himself high as good, if not better than anyone.

Once he opened the door he was a little happier with who it was. It was Martin and Shelly. Martin and Shelly was also on the same play that Clint and Maria met at. The four of them had become rather good friends. Shelly was the type of girl that Clint would have loved to be with. She was a bubbly quirky, funny, nice, girly girly. Sorta like Zooey Deschanel without the talent. Martin was a good guy for the most part. He had that smart ass thing about him. But he could be very funny at times. Overall, they were what some would call "good peoples."

"Clint!" Shelly greeted him excitedly as she ran and hugged him. "How have you been?"

"Oh you know, I take it one day at a time." Clint replied as though he had a terminal illness.

"Damn, this place is kinda the shit." Martin observed. How did you afford it?

"Credit card apparently." Clint responded.

"Ah, that works beautiful." Martin said.

"Well, come in." Clint quipped.

They walked in and were even more impressed than before. If was as if they couldn't believe that they pulled out all of the stops for this. It actually wasn't as if, they couldn't believe that they pulled out all of the stops.

"Why don't we just throw a rager?" Clint asked really wanting to just do away with the dinner party nonsense.

"Ask the lady." Clint said.

"We could really tear it up here." Shelly remarked as she looked around. "I mean tear this shit up."

"There will be no tearing of any shit." Maria said as she marched in.

"Hey!" Shelly said trying not to be fake as she rushed over to hug Maria.

Maria and Shelly had a complicated relationship. Being actors, actresses, performers, and whatever you want you to call it is a tough deal. And this lead to unspoken competition. Both Maria and Shelly were the same types. White, 20s, black hair (though Maria had just dyed her hair blonde), and 5'7. They were constantly auditioning against each other. And Shelly was usually the more successful of the two.

"How have you been?" Maria asked making sure that those acting lessons paid off.

"Oh, ya know well." Shelly replied quickly tried to hide the fact that she's gotten a new role.

"I heard about that new role that you got." Maria said making the guys shiver just ever so much."

"Well..." Shelly said trying to think of a response that could defuse the situation. "It's not really that big of a deal."

"Nonsense." Maria quipped. "Anytime anyone gets a role in this town it's a big deal. "Congrats."

This shocked Shelly. She wouldn't have pegged Maria being able to be happy for her success or anyone else's success for that matter. It was of course entirely possible that Maria was faking it. She is an actress after all. And she wasn't missing out on certain roles because she was no good so much as Shelly was better. So she could have been just acting to not look petty. But Shelly preferred not to think that way.

"Everyone should be arriving soon." Maria said. "Make yourself at home. "I've got to put the finishing touches on the room."

"Will do." Martin said in a sort of weird way. Maria gave him a weird smile as she walked away.

"So, do you guys want to guy want to get high?" Clint asked just being nice. He preferred getting high alone.

"Sounds great!" Shelly excitedly replied.

"I'm good brah, I got to take of something real quick." Martin said.

"Well, if you want to join us." Clint said still just trying to be nice.

Out on the balcony, Clint and Shelly started sharing the bowl. Clint actually liked to smoke with Shelly. She kind and chilled. She didn't bother him like Maria bothered him. She was just so much cooler. Way more low maintenice. Just more confident. She didn't have to put on airs. This was why she was more successful in the audition room than Maria. She was very comfortable in her own skin. She could be herself.

"You just want to get out of it don't you?" Shelly remarked.

"I've been hoping that some helicopter will pass by so I can wave them down to save me." Clint said actually half serious.

"Why do you think Maria does this?" Shelly asked.

"She wants to show the world that she's something or something." Clint replied. "Something like that."

"But who cares?" Shelly asked.

"That's what I've been telling her." Clint said.

"And she doesn't listne to you?" Shelly asked.

"She tells me to stop being a hater." Clint responded.

"Hater?" Shelly said trying to think if that actually fitted into being able to be called a hater. "But you are telling her that she doesn't need it!"

"I guess she's used to so many haters that anyone that says anything that she doesn't agree with is a hater." Clint said.

"We should just be drinking, playing music, smoking weed, and maybe a smidge of cocaine." Shelly suggested.

"I wish you would have thrown the party." Clint said.

"I'm not interested in putting on airs." Shelly said.

And this had to be what attracted Clint to Shelly. She wasn't interested in trying to make herself look good. She was who she was and you would have to deal with it in your way. How could one not become enthralled with an individual like that?

Meanwhile back inside Maria was in the bathroom. She was applying her makeup. She was a very beautiful woman no doubt. But she just had to lay on the war paint. She couldn't imagine having a certain amount. And tonight of all nights everything had to look good. She had to look her best no matter what. There was a knock on the door.

"Who is it?" Maria asked feeling a little embarrassed.

"Yo, yo, yolo." Martin said in a weird voice as he opened the door.

"Ssh, what are you doing?" Maria asked quickly shutting the door.

"Just had to see you in private before this night began." Martin said as he got closer and went in for kiss.

"Cut it out!" Maria snapped. "Are you out of your mind?"

"I'm not the one throwing some dinner party that I can't afford." Martin quipped.

Maria slapped Martin on the face. It was the kind of slap that one regretted giving shortly thereafter. But this party was a soft spot for her. She didn't only want to throw this party, she had to throw this party.

Maria and Martin been having an affair for a while. They both had the same narcissistic flavor. So it made sense that their partners drove them into each other arms because they couldn't get their fill there. But Maria didn't want to mess with that tonight for obvious reasons.

"Look, I just want this night to go smoothly." Maria explained.

"I get it." Martin said as he got himself together.

"So please, just don't." Maria said. "Wait for me to leave."

Maria walked out and shut the door. Martin stood there regrouping. He was starting to really become attached to Maria. He liked her take no bullshit attitude. She liked how she was willing to be a bitch to him. Shelly was too chilled. It's not that he liked being treated like shit. But he liked how different it was from how Shelly treated him.

The doorbell rang once again. Robert started walking towards the door. Maria followed and caught Clint and Shelly out of the corner of her eye. She noticed them smoking. She did not approve of weed.

"Just what are you two doing?" Maria barked as she walked towards them.

"Just lighting up." Shelly answered while Clint tried to hide.

"Clint, what the fuck?" Maria said.

"C'om Maria, it's just weed." Clint pleaded.

"Can't you just not smoke for one fucking night?" Maria asked with anger.

"I have to fucking sneak around because of you!" Clint exclaimed.

"Just fucking chill, more guests are here." Maria said as she gathered herself up. "Finish that shit and come in."

Maria went back inside the greet the rest of the guests. Clint stood there with anger. He was tired of how Maria had been treating him. But he just did not know what to do at this point. Shelly could sense this. But it wasn't her place for her to say anything. And she knew this.

"Let's go in." Clint said as he finished the bowl. And they walked in.

There was suddenly ten more people in the room. Jake, Carroll, Billy, Kelly, Burt, Becky, Harrison, Janice, Kris, and Felicia. All types of yuppies. This is what Maria had been waiting for. She was ready to go out and strike a pose for the world. And she'd like to see anyone try and stop her.

"Welcome, welcome!" Maria said. "I am so that all of you could make it. "Tonight's dinner will be amazing. "As you can see, Clint and I pulled out all of the stops. "Right this way."

Robert guided everyone to the dinner room. Once in everyone was amazed. It was a beautiful room that had the beauty of the dinner room from Beauty and the Beast. Only smaller. Never the less it was extremely impressive. And what through all the guests mind was that "was it worth it?"

Dinner began to get served. A nice four-course meal that included dessert. The red wine out was some of the finest wine available. Clint and Shelly were beginning to get crossed. Weed and alcohol went well together in general. But weed and red wine were just about a perfect match.

"So Martin, you and Maria were out of the country for a while?" Maria asked.

"Ah yes, indeed." Martin replied. "We were in Barcelona. "And it was spectacular." Summer nights there are so warm and beautiful. "The architecture is astounding to look at. "It's impossible not to admire it. "The land is marvelous. "Shelly and I would simply bathe in its beauty. "The food was simply to die for. "Spanish people have got it right. "I...."

"Sounds nice." Maria interrupted. She was just being polite when she asked Martin about their trip. She didn't really want to know about all of the details.

"What about you Felicia?" Maria turned and asked. "You were in Vegas for your 21st birthday, correct?"

"Yeah!" Felicia said.

Felicia was the youngest girl there and perhaps the most bubbliest of all. She had finally turned 21 and lived her dream of going to Las Vegas. And she was just waiting for someone to ask her about that trip.

"How was it?" Maria continued.

"Oh, it was just awesome." Felicia said more than likely overstating the trip. "The drinks were amazing. "The lights were amazing. "The food was amazing. "Gambling was hard. "I lost a lot of money. "But Kris has it covered, right Kris?"

"Yeah sure." Kris responded with anger stemming from having to pay for Felicia's mis steps.

"Well, that sounded, awesome." Maria said.

"How's your movie going Shelly?" Clint asked.

Maria instantly went into a bitch face and instantly tried to hide it. Weed and red wine were just the perfect mix for Clint to attempt to start some shit it. He knew what would really tug at Maria. Hearing about someone who was truly doing something that she wanted to do.

"Oh, it's fine." Shelly said. "No big deal."

"Aren't you the star of the film?" Clint continued.

"I mean yeah." Shelly said. "But it's just an Indie film."

"Just an Indie film?!" Clint remarked. "That's still amazing!" "Maria would kill to be in that!"

Maria started to tremble. She couldn't believe what Clint was doing to her. And for the life of her, she couldn't understand why Clint was doing it to her. She felt that she was the perfect girlfriend and always treated him right. She didn't get why he would start being so mean to her.

"What the fuck Clint?" Maria asked with deep anger.

"What?" Clint responded with attitude.

"What pry tell are you trying to accomplish here?" Maria inquired. "Why are you trying to ruin my dinner?"

"How exactly am I trying to ruin your dinner?" Clint asked holding back laughter.

"You know exactly how." Maria quipped. "Why are you being such a jerk?"

The whole table began to grow rather awkward. No one really wanted to be around any of this. Everyone began looking down and their food and drinks as if they were engaged in an eye staring constantly.

"Maria, calm down." Clint continued. "Do you need your Prozac?"

"Shut the fuck up!" Maria erupted!"

"It appears as though you do need your Prozac." Clint said.

"Clint..." Shelly softly said.

"I try to do something special, and you come along and try to fuck it up!" Maria yelled.

"What is so special about this?" Clint asked. "Please explain."

Maria looked at her glass of wine and an idea stroke her. She picked up the glass and decided to throw the wine on Clint. Clint's reflexes were still quick despite being inebriated and was able to get out of the way. So the wine ended up staining the carpet. And she knew that this would cost her a good bit of money.

"Fuck!" Maria yelled as she threw the glass down on the ground and walked out of the room. Everyone stared at Clint as he continued to eat his food.

"Hey buddy, what happened there?" Martin asked with concern.

"What do you mean?" Clint asked, sounding delusional.

"You two just had a colossal fight." Martin noted. "And you wouldn't let up."

"I was just making conversation." Clint said. It was clear that being under the influence allowed Clint to speak freely. Just not in a nice way.

Maria was now on the balcony looking down to the ground. She had never been so embarrassed in her life. She didn't even see it coming. She didn't realize just how much contempt that Clint held for her.

She didn't realize that she had pissed him off so much. That she was just making everything look better than it really was. And that was what embarrassed her the most.

"Hey." Shelly said popping in.

"Hey." Maria said very softly.

"Clint is just high and a bit drunk. I'm sure that he didn't mean anything by it." Shelly assured Maria.

"Or it was the truth coming out." Maria said.

"Don't think about it." Shelly said as she continued to attempt to make her feel better. "Look at the party that you've thrown. "This is amazing."

"Amazingly expensive." Maria said in a self-defeating way.

"Why do you do this to yourself?" Shelly asked.

"What do you mean?" Maria asked in return.

"Why do you act like you are some sort of piece of shit?" Shelly asked in a very honest way. "You act like you are worth nothing when you are worth so much more."

"Because my career is shit." Maria explained taking Shelly aback. She never really could tell, but it made sense. Shelly's career was going so well. Maria's was not so much.

"Maria, you've got to put an end to all of this." Shelly said. "You are doing fine."

"I don't star in movies like you." Maria responded.

"But you will!" Shelly said in a very comforting way. "Every star arrives on their own time!"

"Enough with the cliches." Maria quipped.

"Look, I may be here now, but it doesn't last forever." Shelly explained. "Nothing does. "I just find it funny how we fill our little lives with things like this that are ultimately meaningless. "At the end of the day, we're all going to die anyway."

There was something about what Shelly said. Perhaps it was the breath of honesty. But it woke Maria up. It made her feel good. She realized just how fruitless everything she had been doing was. Not just the dinner party. But her career, relationships etc. There was no point to them. So there was no point to stress over them.

She gave Shelly a big hug. The two of them shared a moment that they never had ever shared. A genuine moment of connection. A sign of real friendship.

"Let's go back in." Maria said.

"Of course." Shelly said.

The two walked back into the hotel room. Things had changed and were going to continue to change. But not in the normal way for Maria. She would know what to do now.

As they walked back into the dining everyone looked on in silence. What could she possibly do? What could she possibly say?

"Clint." Maria said.

"Yes?" Maria answered.

"I have to be honest with you. "I've been cheating on you with Martin." Maria revealed.

Everyone was shocked. Clint made this face that was mad, shocked, and sad all at once. Shelly couldn't believe what she just heard. And Martin didn't know if he should run or jump.

"Come again?" Clint said.

"Maria, what are you doing?" Shelly asked.

"Shelly, what you said got me thinking." Maria stated. "You are right." So I'm just going to adopt a fuckits mentality."

"So, you've been fucking my boyfriend?" Shelly said. Martin wanted to jump now.

"Maria, why?" Martin asked.

"Because I am tired of putting on these masks." Maria explained. "Time to take them off. "Feels so freeing."

"I love this." Burt said.

"You fucking slut." Shelly yelled at Martin.

"You've got to be fucking kidding me." Martin said.

"I think that we can all finally just be honest with each other." Maria said. "We can all breathe in the fresh air."

Maria knew exactly what she was doing. She now felt that she had license to say what she really wanted to say. She didn't care if anyone thought that her life was neat and tidy anymore. She was just going to be her and she liked that.

Shelly throw a wine glass right at Martin's head and narrowly missed. She then stormed out with Martin running behind her. She was also his ride and they lived in Burbank. Clint had no idea what to do. All he knew was that he wanted to punch something really, really, really hard. He sat there in silent shame.

"So let's get back to dinner shall we?" Maria suggested.

Maria sat back down. She began to eat her dinner. Everyone watched in horror. No one knew what to say. She looked up and saw this as she took a sip of her wine.

"Relax." Maria said. "We're all going to die anyway."

My Life as a Black Cat

"Ι'Τate! Time to get up!" My mom yelled. It must have been 7 am in the morning. Why does school have to be so early? Fourth grade is hard enough to begin with. Having to get up early does not make this an easier task.

I walk to school through the same path every morning. There is a nice short cut that I use. It's very illegal. But it's quick as it cuts through directly to the school. It's the backyard of someone who I don't even know. I would imagine that if he or she saw me that he or she would be none too happy. They would probably sic their dog on me or something. But that hasn't happened yet.

This was the best part of my day. I hated school for several reasons. Of course, it was boring. But I hated the kids at my school. They were not nice to me. People who I thought were my friends ended up turning their backs on me. Treating me like I was nothing. I was constantly teased. The girls just seemed so stupid to me. I couldn't really find any reason to get excited for school.

I hated having to line up outside of the classroom every morning. I would just have a head start on hanging out with kids that I didn't like. I felt so out of place there. If I spoke, I would get an attack be it direct or indirect. If it weren't for the hall monitors, I would have wandered the halls more.

But they would never allow it. I would love to become a hall monitor one day. But I know that they would never allow that either.

I got in line and sat down. I would try and not talk to anyone while sitting there. The other kids just made me feel so out of place. I figured that if I said nothing then it would be as if I wasn't there.

And then I saw her. She had nice brown hair and pretty blue eyes. Her smile was kind and innocent. She walked in such a graceful way. I had my first kiss in kindergarten. I had found out girls to be pretty. But this was the first girl that I actually liked. And wow! What a feeling that was!

All of a sudden, hope came over me. It felt weird. I usually just associated school with pain. But I began to see it a bit differently. Could there perhaps be more of an upside to school? Could something good come out of going here?

The only thing was that she wasn't in my class. So there were still hours in the day that I couldn't see her. And I just found this dreadful. I actually find my teacher nice. She does a good job in class. But it is still school so it still sucks.

But this did allow me to think a little bit about my plan of action. What was I going to do? How was I going to get her attention? Would she even want my attention? Who would want my attention?

"Hey Tate," said Kyle as he walked over to me. "What's going on?"

"Huh?" I said as I stopped myself from continuing to day dream. "What is it?"

"Ms. Katz gave us a project to do and I thought that we should be partners," Kyle said.

"Oh, sure," I replied not really caring. I was just trying to make it to lunch to see her.

"Great!" Kyle said with strange excitement. "Let's get started!"

I didn't really care about the project. It's not like any of this mattered. I just wanted to go and see her. I started to realize that I should probably know what her name is. But that is only a minor hurdle. Once that is accomplished, I would be on my way.

Lunch time hit. If it's not pizza Friday then lunch sucks. It was Sloppy Joes day. Their Sloppy Joes sucked like nothing else except for a pig's mud station. I don't have one common place that I sit down during lunch. I suppose that I am a drifter that way.

I sat down next to Kevin and Larry. And there she was right in front of me. She was digging into that Sloppy Joe. She made it look good.

"Hey, guys. Do you guys know what her name is?" I said as I pointed to her.

"Yeah, Zoey." Larry said.

"Zoey," I said with lust.

"Why do you care?" Kevin asked.

"No reason," I said trying to hide my intentions. "I've just never noticed her."

"Do you like her?" Larry asked bluntly.

"What? Uhh, uhh, shut up," I said not making myself look any less guilty.

"Tate, are you crushing on Zoey?" Kevin asked.

"Just stop guys," I said. If I wasn't black I would be blushing right now.

"You want to hug her, you want to kiss her, and you want to lick her," Larry said basically taking inspiration from Miss Congeniality.

"Just shut up," I said as the recess bell rang. I ran off with relief and excitement.

My opportunity to go and speak to Zoey was finally here. Here was my chance to do something. I saw her on the soccer field. Wow, she was always doing something cool. What do I do now? How can I get her attention?

I had to play soccer. Luckily, I was a pretty good soccer player. I had played for two years straight. Here was my chance to create some wow moments and woo her.

I ran over to the soccer field. I figured that if I were on the same team as her that I would have more of a shot of impressing her. I was starting to tremble. My knees were beginning to shake. I was nervous. I just about wanted to back away. But I couldn't. I had to do this. I had to do this in the name of love.

I walked over to Zoey. Caroline and Lucy were right next to her. Half the team were girls. Usually this would bother me. But today it didn't matter. I just had to get to Zoey.

"Hey, can I join your team?" I asked.

"Why?" Caroline asked rudely.

"Because I want to play," I replied back with a slight attitude.

"You never want to play," Lucy said. It was starting to appear as though they somehow knew what I was up to and were attempting to conspire against me and my quest for love.

"Well, I want to play today," I said commandingly. That should do the trick.

"I don't know," Caroline said.

"What don't you know about?" I said beginning to lose my patience.

"I don't know if we really need you," Caroline said.

"Come on guys!" Zoey said coming in and saving the day. Maybe she felt the same way about me.

"You don't realize this, but not only do you want me, you need me," I said with extreme confidence. This had to have gotten me brownie points.

I could tell that Caroline and Lucy wanted to object to this. But combined with my suave ways and Zoey edging them, they gave me the pass. The plan was now in place ready to go! I went up to Zoey to make my first move.

"Hey, we're going to win." I told her trying to stop myself from shaking.

"Yeah," she said as she ran off. So cool.

The game began. It was such a quick start. I knew that I had to prove something to the team, particularly Zoey, Caroline, and Lucy. On the team was Harris, a kid that I could not stand at all. I had a lot on the line. I had to make some moves.

I started and never stopped. I knew that I would do best as an offensive player. And I did the most with that. Most soccer games in general have little scoring. I scored two goals right off the bat. No one saw this coming. Caroline's and Lucy's faces dropped. Zoey smiled with surprise. Harris and his teammates looked upset. It was on.

The game continued. They could never get a goal on us. Even when they got close, I would steal the ball and score. I was on fire. Was this sexual transmutation? Was Zoey inspiring me to be a great player? When you are playing this good, soccer is a blast.

Right as the bell rang, I scored the sixth goal of the game. We won in dominant fashion. Six to nothing. I was a hero. Everyone came to me. Caroline and Lucy began to kiss me. But I didn't want their kisses. I wanted to know where Zoey was. I could see her in the distance. Smiling with pride. I began to walk over to her when something awful happened.

Harris pantsed me.

He was madder than hell that I had won. And I suppose that he couldn't take it. So he pantsed me. So, there I stood with my pants down. Shame was overcoming my body. I couldn't believe this. On my big day of impressing the girl of my dreams, my pants were down. I felt like I had left this world and then entered another dimension. Erie chills went up my spine. I pulled up my pants and ran away.

I was so mad. I should have just punched Harris in the stomach. Perhaps, I would have saved a little face. But I didn't even think of that. It was like that Linkin Park song. I wanted to run away and never say goodbye.

As I approached the door I heard faint yelling. I turned and it was Zoey.

"Tate!" Zoey yelled as she ran over to me. "Wait up!" I couldn't believe that she still wanted to talk to me after my humiliation of the third kind. Unless she just wanted to rub it in. This was a distinct possibility.

"Harris sucks," she said as she got to me.

"That was so stupid. I was going to punch him in the stomach, but I didn't want to make him cry in front of everyone," I said doubting that she actually believed me.

"I could see that happening," she said with such a pretty smile on her face.

"You know what made me play so good?" I said setting up my major move.

"What?" She asked with real curiosity. It was working out after all.

"You," I told her as her face lit up.

"Seriously?" she asked trying to hide her excitement.

"Yeah, I wanted to get your attention," I told her. "And it motivated me all the way to the win."

Zoey then went in and gave me a huge hug. It's hard to describe what kind of hug it was. It warm and embracing. And she then gave me a nice kiss on the cheek. I got somewhere!

"That is so sweet," Zoey said to me. "We should hang out."

"Yeah!" I said letting my excitement fully go for once. "That sounds like fun!"

"We'll set it up," she said in her normal cool way. "See ya around."

She walked away back into the school. I stood there in a glow. I couldn't believe what had just happened. From zero to hero back to zero and back to hero. It was amazing. I still got the girl of my dreams.

I smiled and held my head up high as I walked into class. Today was I finally on top. And it felt good.

Condon

"Is it on?" Cameron asked Jay as he fiddled with a camera. It was a Nikon D3100. It was a sort of special occasion. Cameron wanted to get laid. But not just with any girl, but with Carissa. Carissa was a beautiful woman. Not in the classical sense. But in every other way. Her hair was black and short. She looked like she was always ready to go to a party. And that attracted Cameron. But Carissa could never figure out what was in it for her. Now he decided to have a nice party at a nice log cabin. Somehow Cameron figured that this would do the trick.

"It is now," Jay said.

"Good," Cameron said. "I'm a bit nervous."

"Why?" Jay asked. "It's just Carissa. Billy and Odette will be here too."

"Don't you understand? This has to work!" Cameron said nearly shaking.

"It's no big deal, man," Jay said trying to become a bit of a reassuring calm voice. "You've got this."

"She hasn't given me the indication of that thus far," Cameron said with his head held low.

Carissa, Billy, and Odette began to come through. Cameron worked to compose himself as Carissa walked up. She made it hard around him. She was so cool and she made him feel like he was so not.

"Hey guys!" Jay said to the group.

"What's going on?" Odette said. "This is a nice place."

"Random, but nice," Carissa said with a skeptical tone.

"I think it will be alright," Billy said with optimism. "It has potential."

"Your positivity grates my brain," Carissa said.

"Hey Carissa," Cameron said.

"Cameron, you're mumbling," Carissa said. If Cameron could blush he would.

"Nice to see you," Cameron said.

"There we go," Carissa said.

"There's some beers and shit in the cabin; never too early to get started," Cameron said trying to sound cool. But Carissa's face conveyed otherwise.

"Cameron, I like it," Odette said.

Cameron began to lead Carissa in as Odette followed. Billy began to walk, but Jay stopped him.

"Billy, want to do something fun?" Jay asked.

"Yeah, what is it?" Billy asked with enthusiasm.

"Work the camera," Jay said. The smile on Billy's face began to sag.

"I don't know, man, that's not really my thing," Billy replied not sounding too positive at the moment.

"You will never know if you don't try," Jay said in full salesman form.

"I just don't use cameras," Billy said trying to politely back away.

"Just take it," Jay said as he aggressively put the camera into Billy's hands. "You'll learn on the fly."

"Jay..." Billy said with discomfort.

"Don't worry about it, brother," Jay said trying to brush Billy off. "Your looking good already."

Jay walked away leaving Billy to his own devices. At first, Billy was a little upset at this. He wasn't interested in this. He wanted nothing to do with the camera. But as he began to play around with the camera, he became more engaged. It was as if a light switch went off in his head. Messing around with the camera became enjoyable to him. And the possibilities seemed endless.

Inside, Cameron was furiously searching for the right drinks to bring out. Carissa and Odette sat patiently as Jay and Billy came out. Cameron just had to make sure that everything was right. The right beer would be a deciding factor on whether or not Carissa would sleep with him. At least in his mind.

He walked out with a bucket filled with ice and craft beers in one hand. In the other, he had a bottle of nice Canadian Whiskey. He wanted to smile ear to ear because of how proud he was in the choices that he made. But he knew that it would look a little off so he stopped himself.

"Enjoy," Cameron said with a bit of swag.

"Oh wow, nice beer," Carissa said actually sounding impressed as she sipped the beer.

"Has a nice tangy taste," Odette said.

"It's one of my favorite beers ever. We'll have to drink it more often," Cameron said as he looked over to Carissa. Carissa didn't quite know what to do with that.

"Let me try this out," Billy said. He was handed a beer and gulped it down like a garbage disposal. "Good shit!"

"At that rate, we are going to need to make another run," Jay said in jest.

"Shots?" Cameron asked. The ideas began to merge into Cameron's mind. If he were to get Carissa drunk, she would be more and more likely to fall into his arms, making his job just a little easier.

"It's early; I want to be awake for this," Carissa explained stalling Cameron's plan.

"Oh, good idea," Cameron said with a bit of dejection.

As time passed on, people started rolling in. It was becoming a pretty good party. It appeared as though a lot of people knew about this and were interested in coming. Drinking games began; people were hanging out by the fireplace. It was all looking good.

Billy decided to explore a little with the camera. He wanted to see if he could parlay this camera into getting himself laid. He thought to himself, "People like directors, right?"

He saw these two girls, Lori and Kasey. Both blonde, both pretty. He walked over there with no idea of what he would say. He figured that he would just wing it.

"Hey ladies," Billy said desperately trying to sound cool.

"Oh, hey Billy," Lori said with slight disappointment.

"What's going on?" Billy asked feeling his way through this. "Enjoying the party?"

"It's cool," Kasey said wanting to get away from Billy.

"You two are chatter boxes, huh?" Billy said hoping to ease the tension.

"We gotta go to the bathroom," Lori said effectively ending what Billy was trying to do. "Later."

"Uh okay, let's drink together later, huh?" Billy asked in a last ditch attempt.

Lori and Kasey walked away leaving Billy alone with the camera. Billy wanted to sink a little with the embarrassment. And he would have, if he didn't see what Cameron was doing with Carissa.

Cameron was attempting to read her palm. This was a trick that Cameron did all the time. And he had become pretty efficient at it. Not effective, but efficient.

Billy walked over to Cameron mid palm read. You could tell that this began to make Cameron a bit more self-conscious. He began to get a bit more stiff.

"What's Gucci?" Billy said ruining things for Cameron.

"Just hanging out with the lovely Carissa here," Cameron said wishing that Billy would go away.

"You going to finish this palm read?" Carissa asked just wanting to see where this was going to go.

"Alright," Cameron said just wishing that this would be over.

He began to rub around Carissa's palm again. If he actually knew what he was doing was beyond Billy and whoever else was watching. Carissa looked at him with half intrigue and half wondering if what he was doing was bullshit.

"You are one tough cookie," Cameron said instantly regretting saying tough cookie. "You got ice water in your veins. But you also have a water heater in your soul."

Everyone looked at Cameron not knowing what to say. It sounded like bullshit. But it also sounded kind of good.

"That was something else, Cameron," Carissa said feeling her way through it.

"Yeah, do I have a water heater for a soul?" Billy said beginning to laugh.

"Billy, why don't you go find some girls and bother them?" Cameron said cutting deep into Billy.

Billy walked away with his head held just a little low. He had been embarrassed two times in a row. All because the camera that Jay had set him up with. This night was just not going right for him. More so than usual.

"Billy!" Odette said as she walked up to him.

"Hey," Billy said a bit melancholy.

"What's wrong?" Odette asked with genuine concern on her face at least. She probably didn't care on the inside.

"I'm just tired of this damn camera," Billy said with angst. "It's holding me down."

"Yeah, I'm sure that you could be in the middle of a three way right this instance," Odette said in a condescending way.

"At least a two way," Billy said as Odette began to roll her eyes.

"Just go with it," Odette said half trying to be supportive.

"Nothing is happening," Billy said dragging himself into further despair.

"Wait and something might just happen," Odette said just about done with this conversation.

She said this just as a loud noise went off outside. It was a loud thud. As if something had crashed. As if something from the sky had crashed. Whatever it was it attracted everyone's attention.

"What the fuck was that?" Jay said scared and nearly shaking.

"Maybe a tree fell," Cameron said.

"Let's find out," Carissa said as she went to the door.

Carissa was a different kind a girl. Most would have made one of the guys do it. But she went right to the door. It made her look like even more of a badass than the usual amount. She opened the door and looked left, then right.

"Looks clear to me," Carissa said honestly believing that.

People were about to continue to party on as another loud noise went off. This had the power of two thuds. And it wasn't a tree. It was a creature. The type of creature that you would see only in nightmares. To describe this horrible creature wouldn't even do it justice. Just know that it looked bad.

Everyone began to run around in a heavy disarray. No one could believe what was going on. And it was clear that no one knew what they should do. Screaming and running around wasn't helping the situation one bit. But of course they continued to do this anyway.

The lights got knocked out in the process making everything just a bit more scary. No one knew where each other was. Suddenly, there was a different kind of sound. A lot more haunting than the ones before. It was a loud scream. A cry for help. Someone was getting ripped apart. Torn to shreds. As some people like to say, it was getting real.

Cameron got to the door and saw Billy who somehow was recording all this the whole entire time. Carissa and Odette showed following the light of the camera and Jay as well. They began to run away all in a group.

As they got outside, they could see that their creature was not the creature that was around. There had been an invasion of some kind. And it was getting to everything. It looked like that ride, *Escape from Pompeii*, in Busch Gardens. There was fire everywhere. Shit was going down.

The group continued to run; Billy was recording this the whole time. The fact that he hadn't dropped the camera was simply remarkable. And the fact that he wanted to continue on filming this whole time was impressive. Perhaps, he felt that if he made it out of this alive that he would have something to sell. That he could make a quick buck or two.

The group ran until they felt it was safe. Of course, they really weren't safe as they were in the middle of the woods where a bear could easily come and tear them to shreds. But the woods felt very quiet tonight. It was as if all of the animals knew what was up and ran away. It gave off a very eerie feeling.

The group began to settle down. They were able to breathe just for a second.

"What the fuck was that?" Jay said not being able to stop shaking.

"Fucking, some kind of aliens," Cameron said still not being able to believe what he saw.

"Whatever it is was, we need to get far away from it," Odette said sounding like she was done.

"We can't just leave them there alone," Carissa said to the dismay of pretty much everyone.

"Why?" Odette asked really wanting to know what her motive was.

"Because it's wrong, we have to get help," Carissa said. She was starting to put everyone to shame.

"Wow, you are so brave, Carissa," Billy said genuinely impressed.

"I know," Carissa said without the slightest hint of cockiness.

All of a sudden, out of nowhere, a girl began running down to the group. She was screaming. She couldn't stop herself due to all of the momentum and hit a tree. The group ran to her instantly. It was Kasey.

"Kasey?" Bill said. "Is that you?"

"Get me out of here!" Kasey yelled to everyone's annoyance. But everyone could understand.

"Just get up," Carissa said commandingly.

Kasey got up a bit embarrassed now knowing that she was a bit safer. She dusted herself off.

"What do we do now?" Kasey asked.

"I don't know," Carissa said. "But we better hurry, their spreading."

This was only the beginning. The world was going to be changing forever.

Only In Dreams

There she was. Who was she? Delicate, beautiful, sweet, and small. Her name was Trish. Trish had a way about her. Only 5'3" yet as much as anyone could have. From the moment that I met her, I knew that something was up. Love? It's hard to pin point. But it must have been love, right?

We had a nice random encounter. I saw her move in across the hall from me. I instantly noticed her lush brunette hair. Her soft snow white skin. Her sapphire eyes. Her thin body. I just had to go over to her and say hello.

"Hi there," I said with a smile.

She looked at me with intrigue at first. And then she warmed up. "Hi," she said back to me with a curious smile.

"Charles. And you?" I asked.

"Trish," she replied.

"Moving day?" I asked. What an obvious question as she had boxes in her hand and through the door I could see the suitcase.

"No, I am breaking and entering someone's apartment," she said. "Not much there."

I could instantly tell that she was the type of girl for me. Outside of her looks, she had a brain and a mouth. She knew how to use it.

"What brings you to this neck of the woods?" I asked trying not to sound desperate.

"I needed a change," she said.

"From what?" I asked.

"I barely know you and you are prying," she said putting up her defenses.

"I apologize. I just want to get to know you," I said trying to make things right.

"That sounds nice. Stop by sometime, huh?" she said with a pretty smile.

She then waved me goodbye and walked into her apartment. I was left with this imprint on me that I just couldn't shake off.

Later that I night, I decided to stop by. I knocked on her door.

She came to the door with her hair all tied up in a hair wrap. Even like that, she looked beautiful. "Hey," she said with a smile.

"I just thought that I'd take you up on your offer," I said.

"Great," she said. "Well, don't just stand there, come in!"

I walked in and took a look at her apartment. It was lovely. Paintings that looked like they were from the likes of David Choe, Van Gogh, and Picasso. On the right was this large canvas with all kinds of paint next to it. She was clearly an artist.

"Are those paintings yours?" I asked.

"Yes," she replied.

"Wow, you are pretty damn good!" I said pleased.

"Thank you," she said with a blush.

"When did you get into art?" I asked.

"As a little girl," she explained. "I walked into an art class by accident. It looked so cool that I didn't leave. So here I am today."

"It appears as though you've done well for yourself," I replied.

"I try," she said.

She walked over to her kitchen and pulled out a bottle of wine. I wasn't sure what the brand was. But it looked nice. She grabbed two shiny wine glasses, poured the wine and served me. I took a sip and instantly I was in heaven. It felt as though I was drinking the highest quality of candy from Germany.

"What do you think?" she asked with a sweet grin.

"This taste amazing," I said.

"It better," she replied, "Cost me $300."

"You spend $300 on wine?" I asked.

"Of course," she said. "Life is too short to not drink good wine."

"How can you tell the difference?" I asked.

"A real wine connoisseur just knows," she explained.

A real cultured woman she was. We continued to talk about whatever entered our minds. It was one of the best conversations that I've had in my life. Three hours passed by and I didn't feel it. But perhaps she did. When she decided it was time for the night to end, she brought me to the door.

"Tonight was great," I said trying to conceal a huge grin from coming across my face.

"I know how to entertain a guest," she said confidently.

"We should do this more often," I said trying to be slick.

"Yeah, my boyfriend loves things like these. He would love you!" she said as my heart crumbled.

My heart instantly sank. I thought she was single. I thought that she was prime for taking. But alas, that was not the case.

"Ah, you have a boyfriend?" I asked trying my hardest to not sound needy.

"Yeah," she said swiftly. "Is that going to be a problem?"

"No, no, no. Not at all," I said trying to sound cool. "Just caught me off guard a bit."

"That's why we moved here. So that he could be closer to work," she explained.

"Oh, sounds good," I said with slight disappointment.

"Until next time," she said.

"Until," I said.

She shut the door and I walked back to my apartment. I sat down in my living room with my face in my hands. I haven't felt this dejected in a while. I thought that I had found a new love. A possible lover. But this was not the case.

I went to bed. Didn't even watch anything and just went to sleep. Dreams are interesting. I sometimes feel like I never dream. At least I never seem to remember my dreams. But tonight was different.

Suddenly, I was in a restaurant. Not as a guest though. As an employee. It felt like I had worked here before. I was in full uniform: a corny hat, red t-shirt, and "flare." Flare was supposed to be our way of showing our restaurant's spirits. The irony here was that it just brought down my spirits.

I looked right, I looked left and it felt like I was seeing people that I met before. But I couldn't put my finger on it. And there she was. It was Trish. She was in the full uniform too. Flare and all. I couldn't believe it. I was so entrenched in this dream that is felt so real. I wasn't quite lucid dreaming. I didn't realize that it was a dream at the time. I thought it was actually happening. It's funny how dreams can work out that way.

"You work here?" I said as she approached me.

"Gotta work, right?" she replied in her sexy smart ass way.

She sat down at the same table that I was at. I looked at her with some sort of amazement.

"Why are you staring at me?" she asked.

"I just can't believe that you're here," I said trying to feel my way through this.

"Well... I'm here!" she exclaimed.

She took my finger and started to slowly play with it. I felt like I was 13.

"Do you think of me?" she asked in a devilish way.

"What do you mean?" I asked trying to make sure she couldn't see the cards that I had laid out.

"You know exactly what I mean," she replied in a sly way.

"Okay," I said not really knowing what to say.

"What would you do to me?" she asked.

"What?" I replied a bit irritated.

"What would you do to me if we were alone?" she asked.

"That is a loaded question," I said.

"Would you just stare?" she asked.

"A little," I said.

She began to tighten up her grip on my finger.

"Would you start to kiss me?" she asked just looking at me.

"Probably," I said truthfully.

"Would you cuddle with me?"

"For a few minutes."

She started to laugh in the cutest way possible.

"Would you try to have sex with me?" she asked. She wouldn't stop.

"I would have to, wouldn't I?" I said.

"Wouldn't you?" she asked.

"I would," I replied.

"What about my boyfriend?" she asked. It felt like 20 questions.

"I would tell him to go fuck himself," I said with confidence not of this world.

"So romantic," she said.

"I do what I can," I told her.

She took my hand and we rushed out of that restaurant. She took me to the edge of this cliff. We were staring at the bright side of the moon.

"Do you love me?" she asked showing some level of insecurity for the first time ever.

"But I just met you," I said trying to sound cool.

"Do you love me?" she asked again with a little more persistence.

"I think so," I said.

"Not good enough," she said.

"I know so," I said, amending what I previously said.

"Then, why didn't you say?" she asked.

"I am scared," I confided in her.

"Scared of what?" she asked.

"Scared of rejection," I told her.

She began to laugh at what I said.

"What?" I said beginning to get annoyed.

"How can you be scared of that?" she asked. "You don't know what I would say?"

"But you live with your boyfriend," I said.

"Not in this world," she told me.

Suddenly we started to fly. I started swinging her around in the sky. I felt so free. I felt so at ease. I felt so good. I never wanted it to stop. We got closer. We looked into each other's eyes. I could see the sparkle in her eyes. We lean in to kiss.

"This is magical," she said.

"I wish that this could last forever," I said with the biggest smile that I've had in years.

"Only in dreams," she said.

"What?" I asked.

Then my alarm went off.

Unfortunately, I was back into the real world. That is the weird thing about dreams. Sometimes they feel so real that you cannot decipher them from reality. And that's the worst part. What if reality is just an illusion and dreams are actually the real world? I need to become a scientist or something to find this out.

I got up in a weird mood. I so wanted it to be real. I so wish it would happen. But I suppose that only happens in dreams.

I walked out of my apartment ready to go to work. And there she was. Trish was on her way out as well.

"Hey you," she said with a big smile.

"Hey, how are you?" I asked.

"Good. Slept like a baby," she said.

"That's good. I'd say the same thing about myself," I said.

"So, when are you coming by?" she asked.

"Umm, I don't know," I said trying to sound like I didn't care.

"How about Friday?" she asked.

"Yeah, that works," I said.

"Great. Well I must fly. I mean get to work. See you later!" she said.

"Yeah, see you later," I said.

She then hurried off. I had to stop and think for a second. She said fly. She said fly. She said FLY!

I wonder if she was dreaming of me.

All The Right Kinks

Red leather boots, blue leather pants, black bra, jet black hair, and blue eyes. That is how she looked. That's what she always wore. She is Gloria Highest, my favorite dominatrix. She worked at Jax, my favorite sex club.

Jax was a place that I could get away from the real world. Get away from my real life. Because my real life was anything but real to me.

I work at Target as a manager and live with my cute, yet annoying girlfriend, Laura. At work, I have to yell at dumbass teenagers all day. At home, my girlfriend wants to wait on me hand and foot. She will cook for me, buy nice wines, and have me ravish her. Sounds nice? It certainly can be.

But it's boring. It's so mundane. It is just the typical relationship at the end of the day. I always thought that when I lived with a woman that the sex would at least be really exciting. That it would be a good balance to niceness of the relationship.

Nope. Everything is the same. I have to smoke weed before sex to even enjoy now.

Then I found Jax. I love Jax because it sets me free. My heart feels open when I am here. I can finally smile

"

naturally when I am here. I have some kind of joy when I am here.

I walk in and sign in at the front desk. The secretary there stares in a way that shows that she is trying to be nonjudgmental. But I am not sure that she accomplishes this.

Without any hesitation, I ask for Gloria Highest. No need to point me to the room. I know exactly where it is. I walk down these long halls. They are painted red and rightly so. I walk into her room. That room is painted blue. Gloria always had darkness to her. I suppose that is the way I like it.

I eagerly await her arrival. I wonder what she has in store for me. Whipping? I am black so while in everyday life, a white woman whipping a black guy is taboo but when expressing a sexual fantasy it's so exciting and breath taking.

Then she walks in. I sit in straight. Class is in session. And it's the most badass teacher ever.

"Hello lover," she says in her usual seductive way. She then starts to walk towards me. She pulls my chin towards her. "How can I get you going tonight?"

"Surprise me," I said with a huge smile on my face. You would think that it was my birthday and I just had the best piece of cake over. But I am about to have the best piece of cake ever.

"You asked for it, lover," she said.

She then slapped me hard. "Get down!" she commanded. I went to the ground. She then raised her boots. "Now, lick my boots!" she commanded. I started licking. I could see where this was going. And I couldn't wait to keep on going.

"Can't you do better than that?" she dominantly asked. "You are supposed to be a good slave. Come on!"

I began to lick more aggressively. I could see a slight smile from her face. I always wondered if she enjoyed this as much as me.

"You love being my little bitch, huh?" she asked. She just always knew what to say. "Get up!" she commanded as she reached for her whip. I quickly got up and she went to her chair.

"Well, get over here!" she yelled. I walked with haste and got on her lap. I knew what she wanted to do. And I was excited about it.

I was about to get one hell of a spanking.

As she started hitting my ass with the whip each hit made me smile just a little more. Every so often I would wonder why I did like this though. Why did this turn me on?

Perhaps, it was giving away control to one person. Knowing that she was not going to really hurt me. Knowing that it was all fun and games. Knowing that I would be okay in the end. And the excitement of it all.

Laura just never wanted to do any of this, ever. She liked to be dominated. Every night, she wants me to take her. Not even in a bdsm way. She might want to be slapped here and there. But usually just missionary and doggy style.

It's nice to have power over a woman. Don't get me wrong. And despite all of this, doggy style is still my favorite position. Might always be. But to have the roles reversed for once is so...refreshing.

As she concludes spanking me, she pushes me off her. She grabs my face and begins to slap me. I love every minute of it. "You have such a slappable face," she says.

I've never thought of it that way. But I suppose I do.

"Get up and follow me," she commanded. I did this of course.

She led me to a spot on the wall where handcuffs were attached. I tried real hard to seal my smile. She started cuffing me to the wall.

"You ready?" she asked with some actual sincerity to it.

I nodded.

She then began to kick me in the balls.

This is perhaps the most extreme way for me to get sexual pleasure. But I can dig it. Each hit releases something other than sheer pain. It's almost relief.

She was good at having fun with it too.

"You gotta stay still," she commanded.

I tried my best.

"Now, you are being a good little bitch," she said as she continued.

Gloria had so much talent. I always wondered how one would get into this kind of business.

The alarm suddenly rang. Our time was up.

"That's it, lover," she said as she started to uncuff me.

I started to feel sad. Not from shame. But from the fact that it was over. And it's always over too soon.

"See you soon," I said as hopeful as a child.

"Of course," she said as she kissed on my cheek. She then walked away in her normal mysterious way.

As I walked out in some pain the letdown continued. I was going to have to hang out with Laura. It would be nice of course.

But I am not always nice.

Does He Know I'm There?

"**K**elsey," Mr. Knight called out.

"Huh?" I said in front of the whole class as they laughed.

"I asked you about the pilgrims," Mr. Knight said.

"Sorry, I wasn't paying attention," Kelsey said.

"Of course," Mr. Knight said as he continued on with the class.

I had a crush on Mr. Knight. And it was bad. Just bad. Even though I was in 11th grade and had some options with guys, I just wanted to be with Mr. Knight.

He was everything that all the other guys were not. Cool, smart, nice. That age is what sold him. He just had experience. All these guys acted as though they knew what was up. But they were in fact oblivious. Mr. Knight actually knew what was up. And he exuded that.

I walked out of class with my best friend, Sarah. She was talking. Saying something that was somewhat interesting I am sure. But I couldn't focus. All that I was thinking of was Mr. Knight. I wanted Mr. Knight.

"Hey Kelsey," Joel said as he walked up to me.

"Oh," I said with disappointment.

"What's going on?" he asked trying to buy himself some time.

"Nothing," I replied. I wasn't giving him much of a chance. But my mind wasn't on guys my age. I wanted Mr. Knight. I wanted to get in there.

"I got to go, Joel," I said admittedly half heatedly.

"Oh," Joel said with slight disappointment. "I'll see you around."

Joel was a nice guy and all. But I wanted Mr. Knight. I wanted a real man.

During lunch, Sarah and the girls, Patricia, Louise, and Kim were all together chatting up about the day's topics. I was buried in my journal. Writing about guess who? Mr. Knight. I guess this is what falling in love was about. A feeling that you just couldn't shake. A feeling that hurt. I had to do something about it.

That next morning, I decided that it was time to make a move. It had to be done right. And I had to look right. No more innocent looking Kelsey. It was time for Kelsey to look like a woman. A woman that would be able to get Mr. Knight.

I applied the makeup in ways that I've never done before. I wore my best looking skirt. It's a good thing that my mom and dad were out the door before I was. They would have never allowed me to get out of the door looking like this.

When I got to school, I got attention like I've never gotten before. It felt like every guy was undressing me with their eyes. It felt weird. But it felt good. The attention was good. Then of course Joel came up to me.

"Kelsey!" Joel said, trying to hide his excitement. "You, you, you look great."

"Thanks," I said having bigger fish to fry.

"You know, there's this thing that I'm going to and I would love for you to..."

"Sorry, Joel, I got to go. Let's talk later."

"Yeah, sure."

I then continued to walk on. Joel stood there defeated. I didn't mean to hurt his feelings. But he just wasn't on my radar. I came with a plan. And I wanted to execute that plan.

Mr. Knight's class was interesting. Of course, all of the guys were looking at me. Sarah kept asking me questions on how I achieved the look. But I noticed how Mr. Knight was looking at me. He had to force himself to look away! He couldn't stop. I had made an impression on him. I had made the right impression. It was working.

After Mr. Knight's class ended I stuck around. "Mr. Knight," I said in the most seductive way that I could.

"What's up, Kelsey?" Mr. Knight asked. Even when he said normal things like that he was so cool.

"I want to talk to you for a second," I said leaning in closer.

"Okay. Go ahead," Mr. Knight said getting a little curious as to what was taking place.

"You are a young guy right?" I asked.

"For a teacher, yes," Mr. Knight replied. "The rest of the staff makes sure I know about it."

"What are you, 24?" I asked.

"Yes. How do you know?" Mr. Knight asked a little taken a back.

"I saw your Facebook page," I replied.

"I thought I had made that unsearchable," Mr. Knight said.

"It's okay. I'm 17," I said.

"Yes, I know, Kelsey. What are you doing?" Mr. Knight asked with suspicion.

I drew in closer to Mr. Knight and finally made the big move. "I saw you looking at me," I said as he gulped. "We should be together."

This clearly made Mr. Knight very uncomfortable. He backed off instantly. "Kelsey," Mr. Knight said with a tremor in his voice. "I am your teacher."

"So?" I asked.

"There are so many things wrong with this," Mr. Knight said as if I didn't know.

"Not if no one finds out," I quickly responded. "And 18 is only one year away."

"This still makes this illegal," Mr. Knight informed me.

"You know about desire right, Mr. Knight?" I started. "Isn't it better that we give into our desires?"

"Yes. Only when appropriate though," Mr. Knight said. This guy was good. He was pushing off my advances like a pro. I am pretty sure this wasn't the first time for him.

"I'm very discreet," I said with a wink of my eye.

Mr. Knight tried to hide it. But he was into me. How could he not be? I was ready for the taking. "Is there somewhere that I can see you out of class?" Mr. Knight said finally giving in.

"Randall's Park is pretty quiet," I said.

"Alright, meet me there at 3 pm," Mr. Knight said.

"Can't wait," I said as I walked out as slickly as I could.

I couldn't believe it! It was working! I was finally going to have Mr. Knight! It was amazing! I couldn't wait for that first touch, that first kiss, that first lay.

I made sure that I was fashionably late. I got there at 3:05 pm and saw Mr. Knight waiting. I made sure to contain my excitement as I walked towards him.

I sat right next to him when I got there. He was more nervous than I thought that he would be. I was a little bit surprised by this.

"I have wanted this for a long time," I said as I got closer to him.

He didn't back away. "You are different from the other girls in your grade, I will give you that," Mr. Knight said.

"It's because I am a woman," I said.

"Maybe," he said.

"I'll show you," I told him. I began to kiss him. He was a bit stiff at first. I suppose that it just took him some time to get used to. Can't really blame him I guess. But he eventually got into it.

"Am I good?" I asked as innocently as I could sound.

"You're great," he said with that famous Mr. Knight smile.

"You just know how to talk to a girl."

We started kissing again. This time with the kind of passion that I have dreamed of. It was just spectacular.

The next morning at school, I was glowing. I'd never felt so good. Everyone noticed. The guys at school paid more attention to me than the day before. I had to brush off Joel twice as hard.

I could get used to this.

I went to Mr. Knight's class excited. I knew I had to hide what we did. But I couldn't help but be giddy. But when I got there I saw a substitute teacher. "What happened to Mr. Knight?" I asked.

"Mr. Knight will be out of the classroom until further notice," the sub said.

Well, I knew what had happened. I got called into the office about five minutes after that. It was like I had been called into death row. I walked to the office with so much fear. I really couldn't believe that this was going down. I just wanted to be with him. How did they find out?

I sat right in front of the principal, Mr. Dill's, office. He called me in. It felt like the longest two feet walk ever. I sat down hearing every sound that was being made in the room.

"Kelsey," Mr. Dill said. "Do you want to tell me something?"

I gulped. "What do you mean?" I asked trying to sound as innocent as ever.

"Let's just cut to the chase," Mr. Dill said. "A student caught you and Mr. Knight being intimate yesterday in Randall Park."

I knew instantly that it was Joel.

"Mr. Knight has been suspended indefinitely," Mr. Dill said.

"But all we did was kiss!" I said.

"That doesn't matter," Mr. Dill replied. A teacher should know better than to get intimate with a student. Even if you were 18, this would have been unacceptable. "Now tell me, did he come on to you?"

"No!" I said. "I came on to him! It was all my fault, blame me!"

"At the end of the day, the adult is the one that holds the power," Mr. Dill said.

I couldn't believe this. Yesterday, I felt like I was in bliss. Now, Mr. Knight's lively hood was being stripped away from him. My parents would freak. My mom would want to sue. My dad would want to kill him. When word got out people would probably think that I am a hoe. But I didn't care. I still wanted Mr. Knight. I don't know why. But I still wanted him.

The 38

"Hey Day Day!" Billy shouted. I am pretty sure that he had gotten his hands on some weed. That is about the only thing that got Billy excited now. It's weird. He loves smoking it. But I think he really loves selling it.

"Day, Day, check this out!" Billy said as I came over.

My real name is David. But my friends call me Day Day. They have been doing this since the eighth grade. Now, we are in the ninth grade and it is still going on. I don't know if I am going to be able to drop it. But it's nice to fit in.

"What's good, cuzzo?" I asked trying to fit it.

"I want you to smoke this," Billy said as he handed me a blunt.

I must say that the blunt was kinda perfectly rolled. I started taking a hit. It was some uber strong weed I must say. I was high after the first two hits. That was my favorite kind of weed. "Good shit, Billy," I said.

"Yeah, nigga. And we are going to push it."

Selling weed was a skill. It is illegal as fuck in Maryland. You get caught with .05 and you get arrested. I didn't want to fuck with that at all. But I kinda did. Billy loved to fuck with it. I think that he got off on it. It made sense when you really thought about it. The danger aspect that was in selling weed was thrilling on some level. I'm sure if you lived in Colorado, you would be able to smoke more weed. But the danger would be gone. It would lose its zest.

Billy and I got into the game because of our mutual love of this zest. Outside of this, living in this neighborhood had nothing to offer us. People wonder why kids go to crime. Try not making places boring to live and we would not have to look for different ways to entertain ourselves.

"Get on that corner," Billy commanded me. "I'm going down Cloverly."

"Aight son," I said. We dabbed up and that was that. It's scary to just stand on a corner and try to sell weed. Don't get me wrong, it's not selling crack. But at the same time, it just gets me riled up. We had green crack, a nice strain of weed. So that was close enough for us.

I see this kid walking by. This might be my chance to get a sale. "Hey, son!" I shouted at the kid?

"Yo," he said as he walked towards me.

"What you about to do?" I asked.

"What do you mean?" he asked.

"You need to get on that wave?" I asked.

"You talking about chiefing?" he replied.

"Yeah nigga," I told him.

"What do you got?" he asked.

I showed him the weed and let him smell it. "This is some loud," he said with some shock on his face.

"Yeah, are you going to buy?" I asked.

"Let me go get some money," he said. He rushed off real quick. I was actually pretty happy. I was about to make a sale. It's always nice when you can do that. Everyone has so many options these days. It's hard out here.

He returned. But he wasn't alone. He was with some big nigga. "Hand over the weed," the big nigga told me.

"What the fuck?" I said. "Fuck you nigga."

Next thing I know, he steels me in the face. I was on the ground. Both of those niggas were beating the shit out of me. I was knocked out cold.

"Day Day! What the fuck, Day Day?" Billy yelled waking me up. "Son, what the fuck happened?"

I looked into my pocket. The weed was gone. 10 grams, gone.

"I got jumped son," I said. "Fuck niggas stole the weed."

"They have to be fucked up!" Billy said. "Come on. We're going to get those mother fuckers."

I didn't even know their names. I didn't know how Billy was going to do it. But he knew a way. He knew who to go to.

We showed up to Kirk's house. Kirk knew everyone and everything about the neighborhood. He was an old head to us, but he was really like 22 years old. The thing was that he had his own resources so to speak. Billy was banking that he would know who fucked me up and over.

Kirk's home was very interesting. It was nicer than you would imagine. He owned art by Jean-Michel Basquiat. It smelled like lemon Febreeze. He was like a soul that belonged in San Francisco or something. But because of money, he was just stuck here like the rest of us.

When Kirk saw us, he was a bit shook up. I must have looked worse than I thought. This began to anger me more and more.

"Yo son, what the fuck happened to your face?" Kirk asked with honest shock.

I looked into the mirror and my face was truly fucked up. Seeing myself just made me more pissed. "Some bitches jumped me and stole my weed."

"Shit," Kirk said. Then he began to think.

"Have you been about some shit?" Billy asked. "Like what punk ass niggas would do this?"

"There is this one kid named Darien," Kirk said. It looked like he had connected some dots. "He and his older brother, Jamal, do this bullshit thing where they trick people and jump them."

"Sounds like you, son," Billy said.

"Exactly," went Kirk.

"Fuck those guys," I said. Now I was really angry. Now I was really embarrassed. I wanted my revenge. I didn't give a fuck anymore. "Let's get them," I said with anger.

"What do you want to do?" Billy asked.

"Kirk, do you have guns?" I asked shocking Billy and Kirk.

"Yeah man," Kirk replied cautiously. "What are you trying to do?"

"I want to get what's mine," I said. "I want my revenge."

Kirk handed Billy and I guns. I don't think that Billy was quite ready for this. He looked apprehensive. I was a bit caught off guard too. I was mad that I got my weed stolen and my face smashed in. But I don't know if I was ready to go full Godfather on anyone.

"Do you really want to do this, son?" Billy asked hoping that I would say no.

"I got to do it, son," I said confidently. "My name is on the line."

In a way it was. I was humiliated and beaten up. Word would soon get around about this. And then people would believe that they could get away with that shit if they did it to me. And of course soon enough people would try to pull that stint on me. And I was not about to have that go down.

In this neighborhood, you had to show what you were made up of. Your reputation is just about the only thing you have to hold on to. If I let go of that, the consequences would be dyer. And I didn't even want to think about those consequences.

"Just be smart," Kirk said like a protective big brother. "Don't go and shoot them in broad daylight."

"Do you know where they live?" I asked Kirk ready to go.

"They around the playground," Kirk replied.

"The bitches are probably smoking the weed," I said. "Come on Billy."

And we were off. We walked down to the playground. And sure enough they were there. "What the plan, Day Day?" Billy asked with fear in his voice.

"Let's talk to them," I said.

So we went up to Darien and Jamal. They were shocked to see us. But they didn't realize that we had guns. They only saw us. They appeared to feel bad. But I think that they subconsciously realized that some real shit was about to go down right here, right now.

"Yo son," Darien said very nervously. "You alright?"

"What do you think?" I said very aggressively.

"Look son, just chill," Jamal said.

"Fuck off," I said. This set them off.

"You serious son?" Darien said as he got up. "Do you want us to fuck you up again?"

"Try you little bitch," I said.

Darien and Jamal started to come at me. I pulled out a gun and shot Darien right in the face. Jamal stopped in his tracks.

"What the fuck are you doing, nigga?" Jamal said.

"Payback is a bitch," I said. Then I shot Jamal point blank. Both were dead.

Killing someone is a very weird thing. To feel the bullet leave the gun and go into another human is a hell of a thing. To watch someone's soul leave their body is insane. I suppose one cannot actually watch the soul leave a body. But you can feel it. And it was, for lack of a better word, a creepy feeling.

"Fuck man!" Billy said. "Did you have to kill them?"

I stood there and thought about it for a second. Then the answer came pretty clear to me. "Yeah," I said. "I think so."

There was no way that I was going to be able to get away with this. I was clearly more fucked than ever. But that was okay. I did what I had to do. And I was okay with that. And once I was in handcuffs, I was still okay with that.

Rock Blvd

A young woman in a Spanish red dress was dancing to a Spanish guitar. Her name was Vanessa. She was short, perky, skinny, with beautiful dirty blonde hair. Richard walked by in amazement. She looked so beautiful. She looked like a dream.

Turns out she was a dream. Or at the least the situation was. Richard woke up to his alarm clock disappointed. That was the third time this week that he had dreamed about Vanessa. Vanessa was his best friend. They had attempted to date in the past. But it just did not work out. So they decided to remain friends. But Richard had been having a hankering for something more. And this created a sense of lack in himself.

Richard lived a normal life. In the morning, he'd fry up bacon, eggs, and hash browns. He went to a nice state school that Vanessa also went to. He was a barista at a nice coffee shop. Everything in his life looked nice on the outside. But on the inside? Not so much.

Richard's first class was Marine Biology. It was an interesting class for him. He dug animals a great deal. He liked the idea of the class. But the class was extremely hard. The professor was a dinosaur. He had worked for Marlon Brando on his island. Apparently, he never once spoke about movies with him. The class was very dense. The exams were tough. Perhaps, the professor understood all this as he had an amazing curve as far as the grades were concerned. What would be a D in any other class was a C plus here.

Richard and Vanessa were lab partners. They were quite a team. She took all of the notes. He did all of the cutting and handling of the creatures. It worked out for both of them.

"I've been listening to this new band," Richard said to Vanessa.

"Cool deal," Vanessa responded. "Who are they?"

"I don't remember," Richard said. "They sounded pretty good so I found some of their songs on YouTube."

"Nice dude," Vanessa said in such a cool way.

Richard was a little bit ashamed of what just happened. He was trying to make himself look cool for Vanessa. But instead he made himself look like a dweeb. He had to think of something fast.

"Want to listen to a song of theirs?" Richard asked.

"Hit me with it," Vanessa requested.

Richard took out his iPhone, went on YouTube and found the song. The song was *Tears for No Reason* by Kristofferson. As they listened, he could tell that Vanessa was being turned on a little by the song. She was impressed with his ear for music. And he's always had a good ear.

"That's a good song," Vanessa said.

"I thought so too," Richard said with a smile. "We should go and see them in a concert some time."

"That would be cool," Vanessa said.

And just like that Richard's confidence was restored. It was probably a stroke of good luck that the professor came in holding a squid in his hand. He didn't have time to fuck up what he said.

Back at his home, Richard was sitting on his couch watching Sportscenter on TV. He found Sportscenter funny. You watch one episode; you've watched them all for that day except for breaking news. But it was so addictive that you had to continue to watch. This was great for people that had nothing better to do with their time other than watch something that is essentially on repeat.

As Richard continued to go into a trance, there was a knock on the door.

"It's open," Richard said.

Vanessa walked in. Once Richard saw her, he got up with the speed of Sonic the Hedgehog.

"Hey!" Richard said slightly surprised.

"Hey you," Vanessa said.

"What's up?" Richard asked trying to just sound casual.

"I was just in the neighborhood and thought I'd stop by," Vanessa said.

Truth be told, Vanessa was not in the neighborhood. She just wanted to see Richard. Like Richard, she had a hankering for getting back into a relationship with him. But she just didn't know how to go about it. She figured that being close to him was better than nothing though.

Richard and Vanessa laid down on his bed. Nothing sexual was happening because neither one of them were brave enough to make the first move. They just listened to music.

"Who are these guys?" Vanessa asked.

"I don't know, let me check," Richard said as he went and reached for the CD. It said Time Troopers. "Some band called Time Troopers," Richard said.

"Ah," Vanessa went. "Never heard of them."

"Some old band that faded, I suppose," Richard said.

They continued to listen to the music when all of a sudden the CD started floating. At first, Richard and Vanessa thought that they were dreaming. But they were clearly wide awake. Then, they started to believe that they were tripping. But they had done no drugs.

"Do you see what I see?" Vanessa asked with great discomfort.

"Yes, and it's not a star," Richard said.

And then they were suddenly sucked into the CD. They were brought into this weird space time continuum where musical notes surrounded them. It was the sort of experience that would be amazing as a ride at Disney World. But in real life, it was very unnerving.

They ended up being dropped into a bar. It was night time. That's all they could really tell. The bar did look retro to them. There was a band on stage. The guitar player looked like Slash.

"Are you okay?" Richard asked.

"I don't know," Vanessa said as she came to. "Where are we?"

Richard began looking around for clues. But for the life of him, he couldn't tell where they were. The place just did not look familiar to him. Though the music sounded familiar.

"I don't know where we are. But that cover band is killing it," Richard said.

A red haired girl came walking from the bar. She wore a leather jacket, spiky boots, and a bright red lipstick. They figured that she would know a thing or two about where they were.

"Hey!" Richard called out to her. "Do you know what the name of this place is?"

"How do you go to a bar that you don't know the name of?" The girl asked.

"We're just a little lost," Richard explained. "I'm Richard, by the way. She's Vanessa."

"Quinn," she said. "And you two are at the Troubadour."

This shocked Richard and Vanessa. They've been to the Troubadour before. And it looked nothing like this.

"Who is the band?" Richard asked.

"Some new band called Guns 'N Roses," Quinn informed him. "They are fucking killing it, huh?"

Now Richard and Vanessa knew that they were in trouble. They were no longer in their own time anymore. Richard looked around and found a newspaper. It was

January 4ᵗʰ, 1986. They had went back in time by 30 years. He showed it to Vanessa who just about fainted.

"Are you two okay?" Quinn asked noticing just how hard that they were bugging out.

"We are just very confused," Richard remarked. This of course was an understatement.

"Is there anything that I can do to help?" Quinn asked.

"We don't know where to go," Vanessa said.

"Hey, I thought that you were mute for a second," Quinn joked.

Vanessa was not amused. "No, just suspicious," Vanessa quipped.

This just made Quinn laugh. "I think I can help you two out," Quinn told them. "Come with me."

Quinn took Richard and Vanessa to a bit of a rundown house. It was one of those one story homes. Not bad just nothing impressive. "This is where my band and I stay," Quinn explained.

"Oh shit, you're in a band?" Richard asked with excitement.

Vanessa caught this excitement and started to become jealous.

"Yeah, we're called Edible Earthquake," Quinn said.

"What a cool name for a band," Richard said.

"That's precisely what I said when I came up with the name," Quinn said.

Richard and Quinn then smiled at each other. They were sharing a moment. This was not what Vanessa wanted to see. Not only were they stuck in the past, she now had competition from someone that appeared to be Richard's perfect girl.

"What do you play, Quinn?" Vanessa asked.

"Just the bass," Quinn replied.

"You slap some bass?" Richard asked very pleasantly. "That is so badass!" The question backfired on Richard.

"Yeah, it's no big deal," Quinn brushed it off.

"How come you're in a band, but live here?" Vanessa questioned. "I mean no offense."

"We just got together a few months ago," Vanessa explained. "It's a pretty good joint. Check it out."

As they got inside, it looked like the inside of a dream that Richard had once dreamt. It was a house that rockers inhabited that was for sure. Joints, beer bottles, guitars, burgers. Yet, it just looked cool. Like an organized mess.

"Rad place," Richard said genuinely impressed.

"The decor could use a little work," Vanessa said.

"That's rude, Vanessa," Richard snapped.

Vanessa was seeing how she was losing Richard. He was starting to get sucked into this world. It made sense. It was everything that he wanted. Rocker chick, rocker home, rocker vibe, the 80s. Didn't get any better.

"We do what we can, ya know?" Quinn said honestly not really caring if Vanessa liked it or not.

"I dig the place," Richard said. "It just feels good."

Quinn directed them to a room where her bandmates were residing. There was Jim, the lead singer/guitarist, Bobby, the lead guitarist, and Greg, the drummer. They made up Edible Earthquake.

"Hey baby doll," Jim said with great charisma. "Who are these fools?"

"Just some friends that I met at the Troubadour," Vanessa explained. "Richard, Vanessa meet Jim, Bobby, and Greg."

"Where are ya'll from?" Bobby asked with a southern drawl.

"Canada," Richard said making it up on the spot.

"Aye," Greg said trying to sound friendly.

"What brings you two from the great north?" Jim asked thinking that it was exotic that they were from Canada.

"We wanted to come to the U.S.A.," Richard explained.

"California is a great place to start," Greg said.

"You all want some weed?" Bobby asked.

"Sure," Richard eagerly replied.

Bobby brought out a plastic bag full of joints. There must have been fifty joints in the bag. All rolled to perfection. Bobby was very serious about smoking weed. It was no joke to him. When he smoked, he was going to be smoking good. He wasn't just going to be smoking some shitty rolls.

Because Bobby had so many joints, he was able to have three joints going. So there are two people per joint. Richard and Quinn ended up sharing a joint to Vanessa's dismay. She was sharing with Jim, who she was not impressed with. She watched as Richard and Quinn talked and laughed with each other. She would touch him when she laughed. She touched him in that way where you could tell that she liked him. Like *liked* him.

Of course, with smoking weed come the munchies. They had tacos. Everyone crammed in those tacos like there was no tomorrow. Everyone that is except for Vanessa. She ate her taco in contempt as she watched Richard and Quinn. She was growing tired of their budding romance. It clearly wouldn't last as they had to go back. But they were getting their eyes off the prize.

Richard was thoroughly enjoying himself. He was loving every minute of it. Quinn was just so cool to him in every way. They rest of the band was a blast too. They were talking about bands that were classic to him, but not too old to them. They spoke about David Lynch and how Eraser Head and Elephant Man were great, how Dune sucked, and how no one knew if his new film, *Blue Velvet*, would be good or not. It was just so interesting to Richard. This time just felt so much more pure to him in every way.

As time passed on, it grew late and everyone went to bed. There was a guest room with one small bed that Richard and Vanessa shared. Richard laid down next to her in excitement over what happened. But Vanessa laid down in anxiety.

"This is just fucking fun as hell isn't it?" Richard asked.

"Richard, keep your eye on the prize," Vanessa barked.

"Eye on the prize?" Richard said with confusion.

"We need to get out of here and back to our time," Vanessa said. "We have no time for fun."

"Alright, dream police," Richard said as he began to laugh.

"I am serious!" Vanessa said. "You are getting way too caught up in this!"

"The way I see it is that we are here now, so why not just enjoy ourselves?" Richard explained.

"Because I don't want to be in 1986," Vanessa said.

The next morning, Richard and Vanessa could faintly hear the sound of drums beating. They crawled out of bed and walked out into the hallway to see what was going on. They looked around and found the band's practice room. They were practicing one of their songs. It sounded fully fleshed out. And very good at that.

Richard and Vanessa stood there and watched. It's not like they have never seen local bands play in their time. But there was something about watching this band play in 1986. Something that made them just feel so pure. They had this way about them. Maybe it was because it was easier to make money in music in 1986. But they didn't seem to care about making money. They just wanted to play.

After practice, Vanessa stood there in the kitchen drinking coffee with Bobby and Greg. Vanessa was trying to think about how she could make small talk. She was impressed by their music. She was impressed by their plight. But she just did not know what to say.

"I have to say I think that what you guys are doing is really amazing," Vanessa stated.

"Huh?" Bobby said confused.

"I think it's amazing how you guys have thrown caution to the wind," Vanessa explained. "How you guys are just going for your dreams. I think that it's so brave."

"It's alright, I suppose," Greg said as he sipped on his coffee.

Richard and Quinn walked in giggling after a morning joint. Vanessa could see that things were just getting worse. They were just starting to like each other more and more. Being stuck in 1986 was just a nightmare to her.

"Hey Vanessa," Quinn said as Vanessa tried to hide her frown. "I was telling Richard about our concert at this music festival. I think you'll have a great time."

"Do we really have time for that Richard?" Vanessa said with an attitude of annoyance.

"I don't see why not," Richard honestly replied.

"It will be fun," Quinn assured. "It's just one big party."

Vanessa didn't want to party though. She wanted to leave. She wanted to get the hell out and be with Richard. She wasn't making any strong moves on him. But she wanted to do things on her own pace. Quinn was working so quickly and so smoothly on Richard that she had no shot at her long game. And she was getting sick of this. But she couldn't just say no.

"Okay, let's do it," Vanessa said.

"You two Canadians are going to love this more than maple syrup," Quinn said as Vanessa rolled her eyes.

The festival was around the Hollywood Hills. When there weren't mountain lions, bobcats, and coyotes up there it was a pretty damn cool spot. It was a great spot for a music festival.

It looked like something that would be in Berkley. There were tents and tepees all around. Someone had their own chimp. It was a bit of a freak show. But just had this freeing, fun, cool vibe going on with it that made it irresistible. You didn't want to get away from it.

Richard, Vanessa, and Quinn walked up the hill together admiring the scenery. At first, Vanessa thought it was a bit too much. But she warmed up to it soon enough.

"Wow!" Richard said with awed eyes. "I can't believe this."

"It's pretty damn hip," Quinn remarked.

"You guys have such a cool thing going," Richard said gushing.

"You trying to make me blush?" Quinn said.

"It's true," Richard continued. "You guys really know how to live."

Richard and Quinn looked into each other's eyes. Vanessa looked on and she had finally had enough of this. Richard had been sucked into this vortex long enough for her. It was time for her to end it.

"Richard," Vanessa said with slight command. "Come over here."

"Just one second," Richard said to Quinn excusing himself.

Vanessa took Richard by his arm and dragged him far enough to where she believed that Quinn couldn't hear them. She was ready to finally let him have it. She believed that his behavior was just to detrimental.

"What's up?" Richard asked innocently.

"Are you fucking out of your mind?" Vanessa barked.

"Relax," Richard responded. "Why are you so upset?"

"Because we need to go back to our fucking time and you are busy there flirting."

Richard was confused as to what Vanessa was doing. But it then started to become clearer to him. She was in fact jealous of what was taking place with Quinn and him. And if she was jealous that meant that she liked him.

"Do you want to tell me something?" Richard asked giving Vanessa the opportunity to come clean.

"I just want you to get your fucking head out of your ass!" Vanessa said.

"Why are you acting like a bitch?" Richard said catching Vanessa off guard. She would have never expected him to talk to her like that.

"Excuse me if I just want us to go back to normal," Vanessa said trying to save face.

"Normal?" Richard exclaimed. "What the fuck is normal to you?"

"How things were before!" Vanessa said.

"Maybe I don't want that!" Richard said. "Maybe I've been looking for something else and I've found it!"

Vanessa couldn't believe what she was hearing. Was he saying that he found something in Quinn that he didn't find in her? Did he want nothing to do with her anymore? He was opening up a whole can of insecurity worms in her.

"What have you been looking for?" Vanessa asked just hoping that it wasn't the answer that she thought it was.

"I don't know," Richard blurted out searching for more words. "I actually just like being around someone that speaks what's on their mind!"

Vanessa then had only one move to make. She lunged in and kissed Richard. She kissed him like she never kissed anyone before. This caught Richard way off guard. He was starting to realize how Vanessa was jealous and was into him. But he didn't think that she would take the plunge. Her lips tasted like blue raspberries.

"Vanessa..." Richard said.

"Just go off with your rocker chick," Vanessa said as she ran away.

Richard watched Vanessa with a bit of sadness. She had finally come clean to him only to go away. It was what he wanted. But things had gotten so confusing. Part of him wanted to go after her. But part of her thought that she needed her space.

Quinn came to Richard, not sure what was happening. She saw the distress on Richard's face. She hadn't seen that type of look on him before. She knew exactly what to do. "Hey, do you want to do, Lucy?" Quinn suggested.

"Lucy?" Richard asked not sure if she had a friend named Lucy.

"Ya know, Lucy in the sky with diamonds," Quinn said.

It's been a while since Richard had done LSD. He liked it. But he was stuck in time at the moment so it probably wouldn't be the best idea in the world to have an acid trip. But he was at a music festival. So fuck it.

He went with Quinn as she took him to a tepee. There were no Native Americans in this said tepee. But it was still rather cool nonetheless. Inside was this guy with the most funky sunglasses that you have ever seen. He carried around this really neat briefcase. His name was Colin.

"What it do, Colin?" Quinn greeted him.

"What it do in the hood?" Colin replied. Richard felt as though he had just went into the twilight zone.

"My friend and I here are trying to get up to the top of the slide, assistance?" Quinn explained.

"No problamo glamo," Colin said.

Colin opened up the briefcase and there were rows of acid tabs. The first row was Yogi Bear. The second was Mickey Mouse. The third was Mighty Mouse. The fourth was Wiley Coyote. The fifth was the Fonz. The sixth was Woody the Woodpecker. And the seventh was Baloo from the Jungle Book.

Richard stared at the briefcase full of tabs as if it were the Holy Grail. He then realized that this was legit LSD. The LSD that he had done was good and all. But this was the real thing. The good stuff. He was about to experience things that no one his age in 2016 could be able to say that they experienced. That created a bit more excitement for him. Now he had to take it.

"I want two tabs of the Mickey Mouse one," Richard said.

"Slow down you crazy diamond," Quinn quipped. "He'll have one tab of Mighty Mouse."

"And that's plenty for you my manny mans," Colin said.

Colin handed Richard the Mighty Mouse tab. He handed Quinn a Woody the Woodpecker tab. The Woody the Woodpecker tab was a bit more head versus body. The Mighty Mouse tab was more of a lighter trip. And a light trip for Richard on this kind of acid would be plenty.

Richard, of course, couldn't feel anything at first. But Quinn held him tight knowing that when it hit that it would hit. And boy did it hit when it hit. Richard closed his eyes and saw the most wonderful colorful patterns ever. Once he opened his eyes, everything just looked super funky to him. This would scatter and then go back into place. He was hearing colors and seeing sound.

Quinn looked at Richard in amazement. She was amused with just how hard he was tripping. He wasn't bugging out. But he was high as a kite off. She was tripping too. But she was so used to acid by now that it was rather controlled. She wishes that she would be Richard right now.

"How are you feeling?" Quinn asked already knowing the answer.

"Did you hear the color red?" Richard asked.

"No, what did he say?" Quinn asked playing along.

"I don't know. But he sounded mad," Richard said concerning Quinn. She didn't want him to have a bad trip.

"Easy there," Quinn said in a very comforting way. "You're okay."

"I don't know, I don't know, I don't know," Richard blurted out.

Quinn turned to Richard and looked him right in the eye. When they locked eyes, it was as though Richard could see God for a second. They began to kiss. Richard liked kissing her. It felt good to him. But it also felt bad. He couldn't get Vanessa out of his head. This was the introspective part of LSD that was hitting him. He knew that he wanted her. And that he had to go after her.

"Wait, stop!" Richard said to Quinn's surprise. "I can't do this."

"Why?" Quinn asked very confused.

"I have to be with Vanessa," Richard confessed.

"Again, why?" Quinn asked still confused.

"We have this thing ya know, she used to be my girl ya know, then we broke things off, now she wants me and I want her, so I have to just go for it ya know?"

"Yeah, I know," Quinn said smiling.

Richard gave Quinn a nice big kiss. He then got up. Hit a few things by accident and rushed out of the tepee. It was time to find Vanessa. He now felt that he had the courage to really go after just what he wanted. And this gave him a strong feeling of freedom. Freedom with the indecision that has plagued him.

Meanwhile, Vanessa was sitting backstage. The band was getting ready to go on stage. They were just waiting on Quinn to show up. Vanessa was trying to get thoughts of Richard out of her head. She was convinced that it was just never going to happen to him. She was not okay with this. But she would have to live with this.

Jim walked by and took notice of Vanessa's face. He saw the sadness and indecision that she was conveying. He wanted to just keep on walking and not get involved. After all, it had nothing to do with him. But he began to feel bad with that thought. So he came over.

"What it do?" Jim asked trying to sound friendly.

"What?" Vanessa responded caught off guard.

"You look like you in some serious deep thought," Jim commented.

"Yes, I suppose one could make that observation," Vanessa said.

"You know when I have to think about something I always do something that frees the mind," Jim said.

"What would that be?" Vanessa asked legitimately curious.

"Smoke a little weed, drink a little wine, and play music," Jim said. Vanessa rolled her eyes kind of mad at herself for not seeing that one coming.

"That sounds very nice," Vanessa said.

"Oh, it's wonderful!" Jim said. "Do you want to come on stage with us?"

"On stage?" Vanessa asked now really caught off guard.

"Yeah!" Jim replied with excitement. "More pretty girls, the better."

"But what would I play?" Vanessa asked partly trying to find a way out.

"The tambourine," Jim suggested.

"Sounds good," Vanessa said as Quinn came back stage.

"And she's here!" Jim said. "Alright, we're on in five!"

Jim ran off to get the rest of the band ready. Quinn walked to Vanessa. The awkwardness between the two could be felt in the air. Vanessa knew even less know than she did before.

"I'll be joining you guys on stage," Vanessa boasted.

"Oh?" Quinn went. "What are you playing? The tambourine?"

"Yes," Vanessa said slightly putting her head down.

"Well, it's better than the triangle," Quinn quipped.

"Let's go!" Jim yelled.

Richard ran into the crowd looking for Vanessa. He figured that she would be around for the Edible Earthquake show. There was more people around for this show than he had anticipated. Music festivals back in the day appeared to be a much bigger deal than they were in his future team.

Edible Earthquake got on stage. To Richard's complete shock, Vanessa was there holding her tambourine. And they began to play a song. It was the same song that Vanessa and he had walked in on them practicing in the morning. And it was even better than that. Vanessa was going at it. Richard had never seen her be so free before.

She looked so sexy on stage. She was dancing around the lead guitarist, playing the drummer, dancing around Jim. Even her and Quinn had a moment. No one could take their eyes off of her.

When the song was over, the crowd erupted into large cheers, begging for an encore. But the band was smart enough to know that it was better to leave them wanting more. Richard stood there, still tripping, in amazement. He couldn't believe what he had just saw. He had to see Vanessa now.

He ran back stage. He saw Vanessa getting off the stage. She was sweating. But she had a glow in this kind of a sweat. She looked as though she had just won some kind of championship or something. She was basking in the glory.

"Vanessa!!" Richard yelled.

Vanessa turned. "Yes?" she replied trying to sound cool.

"That was so cool!" Richard said sucking up.

"Yeah, I thought so too," Vanessa quipped.

"Why are you acting like that?" Richard asked.

"Oh, what do you mean?" Vanessa asked continuing her deadpan streak.

"Are you still mad at me?" Richard asked.

"Oh, please Richard," Vanessa said. "Get over yourself."

"Okay Vanessa," Richard said as he walked away.

Vanessa looked on as Richard walked away with this bittersweet feeling. She felt cool in a way. But she felt disappointed in herself in a way. He appeared as though he was ready to do something with her. And she had just thrown it away. And that made her feel like shit.

Later that night, everyone was back at the house. Richard sat there on the doorsteps. The acid still lightly loomed over him. The trees continued to wave at him. He was stuck in 1986 and his situation with Vanessa had only grown worse. Why was he here? What was the purpose of all this?

Quinn walked out with a blunt in her mouth. She was still basking in the glory of a show well done. She noticed the look on Richard's face. This was the first time that she really saw him upset. She knew why of course. Part of her didn't want him and Vanessa to get together. But she did like Richard, so she wanted him to be happy. It was just a matter of fighting off the selfish part of hers.

"Blunt?" Quinn suggested.

"Why not?" Richard replied taking the blunt from Quinn.

"She is way into you," Quinn assured Richard. "I mean WAY into you."

"Looks can be deceiving," Richard said in a very self-defeating kind of way.

"Yeah, she puts on a front. But really it's about insecurity," Quinn remarked.

"Vanessa is too cool for that," Richard said.

"That's a part of the front," Quinn informed Richard. "She makes herself look that way. And she almost does a good job."

Richard sat there and let that digest. He began to see just how right she was. Vanessa wasn't as cool and confident as he believed. She was actually quite neurotic. Way more than him. While this realization may have become a turnoff for most guys, for Richard it just made Vanessa more attractive in his eyes.

"That makes sense," Richard said. "That actually makes perfect sense."

"The chick is into you. Probably more into you than you are into her," Quinn continued.

"I don't think that's possible," Richard said.

"Why?" Quinn asked with real honesty. "You are a hell of a catch."

Richard and Quinn shared another moment. In another lifetime they would be lovers. She was the type of women that he had dreamed of. But alas, it wasn't meant to be. His heart belonged to Vanessa.

Richard gave Quinn a nice warm hug. He took one last nice drag on the blunt. The kind of drag that you took when you about to do something big. Like a bold move. He went to the back and started looking for Vanessa. He knew exactly what he had to say now. And nothing was going to stop him.

Vanessa was in the back in the makeshift hot tub. She had drank just a little bit and was floating off in her own universe. She didn't see Richard walk towards her so he caught her a bit off guard. There was nowhere to hide. She didn't know how to react.

"Oh hey," Vanessa said somewhat like a mouse.

"We need to talk," Richard said in a take charge way.

"Okay," Vanessa said as Richard climbed into the hot tub.

"Look, I like you, you like me. "What the fuck are we doing?" Richard said. "Don't you think that it's time that we cut the shit?"

Vanessa couldn't believe what she was hearing. Richard was really coming clean to her. She never thought that this day would come. She tried to hide her emotions a bit. But she was too over joyed for that.

"I've been waiting to hear you say that," Vanessa said.

"Good," Richard said. "And I will be saying more things such as this from now on. I think it works."

"It's sexy," Vanessa said.

Richard and Vanessa stared into each other's eyes. They hadn't connected with each other this way in a long time. They could feel each other's vibrations like never before. And it felt so harmonious and joyful. They began to kiss. Their kissing might as well be mountains moving with the way that they felt. Never before had things been so clear. Never before had things just made so much sense. Of course, their kissing led to sex. There was no stopping that. Neither one of them has had sex in a hot tub before, so that was a bit of an adjustment. It wasn't as fun as they thought it would be. But it felt good. It made the occasion unique. That and being in 1986.

They ended up making it to the bedroom and went at it for as long as possible. Then they fell asleep in each other's arms. Both puckered out from the intense love making sessions that they had both undertook. They had ravished each other and had finally been able to be honest with themselves.

As Richard awoke the next morning, he could sense something was different. He looked around and then realized that he was in his own room again. But he wasn't so sure that this wasn't just a dream. He explored the apartment and realized that, in fact, this was their apartment. They were back! They were home! Richard ran to Vanessa with great haste. He had no idea what had brought them back. And at that particular moment in time he could care less. "Vanessa!" Richard yelled. "We're back!"

"Huh?" Vanessa said in a blurry way.

"We are back!" Richard yelled once again. "We are here!"

Vanessa looked around. She started noticing that this was Richard's room. She looked outside the window and remembered the surroundings. She looked in the hallway and it all was the same. They were, in fact, back.

"But how?" Vanessa asked.

"I don't know. And quite frankly, I don't give a damn," Richard remarked. "I am just happy to be here with you."

"Good answer," Vanessa said leaning in for a kiss.

Perhaps, it was just time for them to come back. Perhaps, it was them revealing their true intentions to each other, letting go of their repression. Whatever it was, it worked. And in most situations, would always work.

Hood Rich

Peter was in a peculiar situation. He lived in Inglewood, California. He grew up in a bit of a hood. His whole life had been surrounded with the same people. But no more. Ever since the NFL decided to come to L.A. things were changing. Everyone was pretty much gone. The neighborhood had become as they would say, "white".

Peter had nothing against white people. There was no reverse racism going on. He just wanted his old neighborhood back. Change was a weird thing to him. And this much change was downright uncomfortable.

One morning, Peter was leaving his apartment to head out to work. He fancied himself a street pharmacist. As he was walking down the stairs, he ran into a woman named Isabel. Isabel was a short, brown haired and brown eyed girl. Peter found her cute. But not cute enough to the point that he'd want to talk to her.

"Good morning!" Isabel said in an extremely friendly and perky manner.

"Morning," Peter replied looking at Isabel as though she had a cow on her head.

"It's always nice to see a neighbor!" Isabel continued. "I'm Isabel, what is your name?"

"Peter," he said.

"I love that name!" Isabel exclaimed. "One day, when I have a son, I want to name him Peter.

"You're smart," Peter said trying to leave.

"Wait!" Isabel called out. "Can I ask you something?"

"What is it?" Peter asked with annoyance.

"So, my two sisters and I just moved in, right?" Isabel started.

"Is that your question?" Peter asked.

"No, silly Billy," Isabel replied. "I have a younger sister who is five. It's summer and we need a baby sitter. I was wondering if you'd be interested in helping us out."

This is not what Peter had expected to happen this morning. When his old friends were here, no one ever asked him to babysit. They could more than likely see that he would not be interested in such a task.

"Lady," Peter started. "You just met me and you want me to babysit your five your old sister."

"Pretty much," Isabel said with a huge smile.

"But why?" Peter asked just trying to figure this out.

"I am a good judge of character," Isabel said. "I can tell that you are a good guy."

She was good with words. And perhaps she was a good judge of character. Peter was certainly not a bad guy by any means. He had a heart of gold. But there has been dust left on that heart for so long that it was hard to see.

"I don't know," Peter said with his indecision hanging there.

Isabel saw this as an opportunity to convince him. "I know that you'd be great with her," Isabel said. "Her name is Sarah."

"Okay, okay," Peter said finally giving in. "Let me meet her."

Isabel took him to her apartment. She actually lived right across him. It's funny how you could have so many neighbors in such close proximity and never even see them. If not for the chance meeting between Peter and Isabel they would have never ever met each other. Their lives would have been radically different as well.

"I didn't realize that you live right across from me," Peter noticed.

"Gotta live somewhere," Isabel remarked. This was true.

Isabel opened the door and out came running Sarah. She was a very cute and energetic five year old. She probably just wanted to get out.

"Hey Sarah!" Isabel said in what was now solidified as her normal perky way. "I have a friend that I want you to meet. His name is Peter. He'll be babysitting you."

Sarah stared at Peter. She hadn't really seen too many people before. So she did not know what to make of him. He stood there and she appeared cool to him. So he started to smile.

"Hi," Sarah said.

"What it do?" Peter said making Sarah laugh.

"I can tell that this is the start of a beautiful friendship," Isabel said.

Just as Peter was going to take Sarah for the day, someone walked out. She had nice blonde hair, bright blue eyes, red lips, pink nails, and sharp red stilettos.

"Peter, this is Teresa," Isabel introduced.

"Hi Peter," Teresa said.

"Hey, what's up?" Peter said gathering himself together.

"Peter is going to be babysitting Sarah today," Isabel said.

"Nice, thank you so much," Teresa said. She might as well be glowing and floating to Peter as he could just not take his eyes off of her.

"Not a problem," Peter said. "Just glad that I can help."

"We've got to go," Teresa said. "But when we come back, you should join us for dinner."

"Damn straight," Peter said. Everyone looked at him as if he were high.

"See ya," Teresa said.

"Thanks Peter!" Isabel said.

And they were off. And then it was just Peter and Sarah. Peter then realized that he had to babysit a five year old girl. How was he supposed to do that? He needed to work too. Why did he give in? The manipulative powers of Isabel got him to do it.

"I'm hungry," Sarah whined. Peter could tell right then and there it was going to be a long day. So he took Sarah out for some ice cream. He figured that Teresa and Isabel wouldn't be too happy about this. But it was cheap and easy. And he could make a few deals while he was out.

"What do you do?" Sarah asked

"I'm a pharmacist," Peter said.

"Like at CVS?" Sarah asked.

"Better," Peter said.

"How?" Sarah asked.

"I am a lot quicker," Peter said becoming irritated. "Now just finish your ice cream."

Sarah was enjoying a nice Rocky Road ice cream. Two scoops. Peter thought that it would be too much to give her three. As she licked, a drug fiend named Kip approached Peter. He walked with a limp and wore his baseball cap backwards.

"Yo, Pete!" Kip said.

"Hey Kip," Peter greeted him. "What can I get you?"

"I need some of that goody two shoe shit," Kip said.

"Right," Peter said.

Peter reached into his pocket for that goody two shoe shit. It turns out that goody two shoe shit was weed. The strain was called green crack. Some of the best weed that was out on the market. Peter was the best weed dealer on the block. His connections grew. So it had that earthly feel to it. But the trichrome on these buds were so abundant. The amount of THC was at least 25%.

"There we go, son," Kip said with glee.

"Let me know when you are trying to re-up." Peter said.

"You already know," Kip said as he skipped away.

"Who was that?" Sarah asked.

"Don't worry about it," Peter commanded. "What do you usually do for fun?"

"Go to the playground," Sarah answered.

"That sounds awful," Peter thought out loud. "I've got a better idea."

Peter decided that it would be a good idea to take a five year old girl to a shooting range. Now, of course, she wasn't allowed to shoot the guns. And really she wasn't allowed to even go in. But, of course, Peter paid off the guy running the thing.

Peter loved to go to the shooting range. It was his way of blowing off steam. He didn't own a gun like most gangsters. He never wanted anything to do with that. But he loved the power that he felt when he held a gun in his hand. He understood why someone would want to own one. It was the best way of telling someone, "Don't fuck with me!"

With each bullet fired something was released into Peter. More than likely, it was just dopamine. But it felt as though it were something more. Like he was really in control of his situation. Like outside factors weren't affecting what he was doing. Like he wasn't just being jerked around. He truly felt alive.

Sarah watched Peter in amazement. She, of course, did not quite comprehend what was taking place. She could feel that Peter was experiencing something. Something that was actually giving off rather positive vibes. "Is this really fun?" Sarah asked in the cutest and most innocent way ever.

"Fun wouldn't even be able to describe what I am feeling," Peter explained.

"Why do you do this?' Sarah asked again.

"Because I need it," Peter answered.

"Why?" Sarah asked.

"I guess that's the million dollar question, isn't it?" Peter replied.

With each bullet fired, Sarah got more and more excited. She was actually starting to grow on Peter a bit. He didn't know what to expect from Sarah. But she seemed to be cool with whatever he did.

Peter also began to feel bad for her too. He was being selfish as far as what they were doing. He wanted her to have fun too. Then an idea struck his head.

Peter decided to take her to an archery field. She was still too young for that. But once again, he paid off the guy working there. He handed her the Bowen arrow that was just about half her size.

"Can you handle this?" Peter asked.

"I think so," Sarah said not entirely sure of herself.

Peter guided her as she pulled back on the arrow and released. She hit the target right off the bat. At first, Peter thought that this was just beginner's luck. He decided to let her go to see what she really had in her. She released and hit the target bullseye once again.

"Wow, you're a natural," Peter remarked.

"What does that mean?" Sarah asked with the sweetest sincerity.

"It means that you were born with a gift," Peter explained.

"I have a gift?" Sarah asked with genuine surprise.

"Of course," Peter said. "You are very special."

"I am?" Sarah asked.

"Yeah, hasn't anyone ever told you that?" Peter asked.

"No," Sarah said putting her head down.

"Well, they should," Peter told her. "You are."

Sarah smiled at Peter. She had never had someone really talk about her in such a positive light. Perhaps, it was because her parents were out of the picture. Perhaps, it was because her sisters were always working. But no one really thought about cultivating her self-esteem. Peter was the first person that showed any interest regarding that.

After all of this, Peter and Sarah hung around the playground. Peter was smoking a nice blunt. Sarah had never smelt weed before. To her, it smelt like a unicorn's arm pit. Pretty, but a distinct scent at the same time.

"What is that?" Sarah asked.

"Something that you should never do," Peter replied.

"Why?" Sarah asked again.

"Because I don't want you to be like me," Peter told her.

"But why?" Sarah continued. "You are so cool!"

"You don't know what cool is sweetie," Peter told her surprising himself that the word *sweetie* came out of his mouth.

"What is cool?" Sarah asked.

"I am still trying to figure that out," Peter said in the most revealing way. "Now, promise me one thing."

"What's that?" Sarah asked with wide eyes.

"That you won't say what we did today to your sisters," Peter told her. "Just say that we went for ice cream and went to the park."

"You want me to lie?" Sarah asked legitimately shocked.

"Yes," Peter said.

"But isn't lying bad?" Sarah asked.

"Only when it hurts someone," Peter explained. "This will protect them."

"Protect them from what?" Sarah continued to ask.

"Protect them from themselves," Peter explained.

Peter brought Sarah back to Teresa and Isabel. Teresa and Isabel were surprised with the big smile that Sarah had on her face.

"Thanks again, Peter," Isabel said.

"I hope that she wasn't too much trouble," Teresa said.

"Not bad," Peter remarked holding back his emotions. "Not bad at all.

"He's so much fun!" Sarah said.

"What did you two do?" Isabel asked.

Sarah turned and looked at Peter. He nodded his head indicating to her not to tell the truth. Suddenly, this internal feeling came upon Sarah. She knew that lying was wrong. But she did not want to make Peter mad. And maybe he was right. Maybe lying was okay if it was protecting someone.

"We went to the playground and had ice cream!" Sarah said.

Peter smiled in relief.

"Sounds like a good time!" Teresa said. "Peter, do you like roast beef?"

"I love it!" Peter said.

"Well, it's a bit burnt," Isabel explained.

"Bring on the ketchup," Peter said with a warm smile.

They all sat around the dinner table as Isabel brought out the roast beef. It was indeed a bit burnt. But ketchup does have a magical way of making things taste a lot better than they really taste. Red wine could also come in handy.

"What made you three move here?" Peter asked.

"It's a long story," Teresa said trying to avoid the topic.

"I've got time," Peter said.

Teresa and Isabel looked at each other. It was as though they were telepathically speaking with each other. They were not sure if they should talk about their reason and tell someone that they just met. But Peter seemed like a nice guy. Sarah really did seem to adore him. They deemed that it was okay to let him in.

"Our mother died," Isabel said. The mood of the table shifted instantly.

"Oh," Peter said feeling bad that was prying. "I'm so sorry."

"It's okay," Teresa assured him. "She was dying of lung cancer. She doesn't have to suffer anymore."

"We wanted to get away," Isabel explained. "So, we came here."

Peter didn't know what to say. All of a sudden, the dinner became heavy. One question suddenly brought in the darkness. He took a sip of wine and started looking around. He could see that Sarah was becoming a little sad. He began to feel more and more bad.

"Ya know, at least she doesn't have to see them waste money on that stadium," Peter said. "Especially for a team that is going to suck."

Everyone began to laugh. Sarah really didn't get what was going on. But she began to laugh because everyone was laughing. Just like that, Peter had just been able to turn it around. This gave him a strange feeling. This made him feel all warm and fuzzy inside.

The dinner continued on. More and more laughs were shared. Peter was able to dissect the personalities of Isabel and Teresa. While not the oldest, Isabel was the de facto mother figure. She worked as a teacher's aide at an inner city high school. She wasn't the most exciting girl ever. But she was good natured. She had good values.

Teresa, on the other hand, was different. It wasn't that she was not a mother figure to Sarah because she certainly was. But in a different way. She was like the cool mom. She worked as a bartender is a great bar in Hollywood. She made a lot of money. For sure a lot more money than Isabel. She took the road less traveled, if you will. She had great stories to tell too. You could tell that she liked to have fun. She was very attractive to Peter.

The night went on and on. Everyone seemed to have a great time. Sarah had to be put to bed so that was the cue that the night was over. Peter couldn't believe it. He did not want to leave. He wanted to stay. Not just with Teresa, but with Isabel and Sarah. He had enjoyed their company. He hadn't felt this way in a long time.

Isabel was putting Sarah to sleep so Teresa showed Peter out. It was clear that there was an attraction between the two. A connection had been built. Both wanted to explore this. But neither knew what to say.

"That was pretty damn great," Peter said with a huge, genuine smile.

"Yeah, it was," Teresa said returning the smile.

"If you need me to babysit Sarah just let me know," Peter informed her.

"Oh damn, I am going to have to take you up on that offer," Teresa replied.

"I'll be ready," Peter said.

The two of them hugged each other goodnight. There was a moment where it appeared that a kiss could happen. That tingly electric feeling was in place. But it just didn't happen. It was like a gun was in someone's hand

and they decided to not pull the trigger for whatever reason.

When Peter went to bed, he went to bed feeling better than he'd felt in months. The connection that he had built with those three girls was true and genuine. Ever since his friends had gotten forced out, Peter had kind of been on his own. And he had gotten used to being on his own. He was beginning to forget what it was like to have a real human connection. Isolation will do that to you. However, with them, he was reminded of the riches that human relationships can bring.

Peter started to smoke his bong. He always had a goodnight toke. It was pretty much a part of his bedtime ritual. But this time, he did it with a different attitude. He was happy before he started smoking weed. The weed was just a bonus.

The next morning, Peter woke up ready to go to work. He had hardly sold anything yesterday due to hanging out with Sarah. Not that this bothered him. But he had to make some bread.

He made his cup of coffee that he drank while he smoked his weed. Weed and coffee just fit so well for him. Then his doorbell rang. He assumed it was a client. He really didn't like having clients come over.

"Who's there?" he asked as he walked towards the door and then opened it.

It was Teresa standing there with Sarah. Both of their eyes were wide eyed and a bit sad. Peter was kind of high at this point so he just stood there and stared at them not knowing what to say.

"Hey," Teresa said.

"What's good?" Peter asked trying to hide how high he was.

"So, there's a bit of an emergency that needs to be taken care of," Teresa explained nearly shaking. "I was wondering if you would take care of Sarah for the day. I know this might be too much."

"No, no, no," Peter said. "It's not too much at all. Anything to help."

Teresa went in and gave Peter a big hug. It was the kind of hug that you gave someone after they did something for you that was so monumental and lifesaving. The kind of hug that showed that you indeed understood this.

"You are an angel," Teresa said. "Be good, Sarah."

Teresa ran off also as fast as Sonic the Hedgehog. Peter was worried for her. Clearly, something was wrong. But he couldn't focus on that. A wide eyed Sarah was staring right at him.

Peter was in a bit of a spot. He really needed to work today. But Sarah was here. Doing one deal around her was fine. But a whole day was risky and downright irresponsible. But he had to do what he had to do.

"What are we going to do today, Peter?" Sarah asked.

"Sarah," Peter started. "I need you not say anything about what is going to happen today."

"What's going to happen today?" Sarah asked a little worried.

"You'll see," Peter told her. "You just can't say anything. Okay?"

Sarah nodded her head and they were off. Peter had to be very careful. He didn't want to poison Sarah's mind. He didn't want her to grow up and become a drug dealer herself. But he had to do what he had to do. It was a rough deal. But he felt that she would be surprised.

Peter and Sarah posted up on the sidewalk. Peter gave her a pair of sunglasses. This made Sarah feel like she was cool. In her mind, she was chilling like a villain. Peter was a bit nervous still. It just didn't"t feel like something that he should be doing. But, on the other hand, perhaps this was just resistance.

All of a sudden, a guy in a nice black car rolled up. At first, Peter had his reservations. The car looked a little suspicious to him. But he couldn't put his name on what it could be. He figured that this is just resistance rearing its ugly head, so he went up to the car.

"Yo," Peter said.

"Yo," The man in the black car said. "What do you got?"

"I've got that loud packy yao," Peter told him.

"How good is it?" The man asked.

'There's a reason why I call it the loud packy yao," Peter explained.

"Can I see it?" The man asked.

Peter brought out the weed. You could smell it from a mile away. It smelt like an orange and skunk had gotten together and had a baby. The man in the car took a good whiff of it and couldn't believe what he smelled.

"You are under arrest," the man in the car said as he pulled out a gun.

"What?" Peter said shocked as hell.

Turns out, he was an undercover cop. What luck for Peter. His first sell turns out to be an undercover cop. Sarah stood there, scared not being able to move. The cop noticed that she was with him and looked at Peter with a certain kind of disgust.

"Is she with you?" The undercover cop asked.

"Yes," Peter said with shame.

The undercover cop shook his head. He handcuffed Peter, got him and Sarah into the car and drove off. He booked Peter and took Sarah into child services. Peter had brushes with the law before. But he'd always been solo. Implicating a five year old girl was just not cool.

Peter sat there in his jail cell with the ultimate disgust. He didn't want to look at or talk to anyone. He couldn't believe what he had just done. He had screwed over Teresa and Isabel. They would never forgive him for this. He didn't even know if he would be able to forgive himself.

A guard came marching in. To Peter's surprise, Teresa and Isabel walked in. They looked more concerned than he would have imagined. But make no mistake about it, they were livid. Peter could feel it.

"You made bail," The guard informed Peter as he let him out.

Peter could hardly walk out before Teresa slapped him hard across his face. Isabel slapped him on the other cheek. Peter knew that he deserved it.

"What is wrong with you?" Teresa asked.

"Drug dealer?" Isabel commentated.

"I don't know what to say,'" Peter confessed.

"There's nothing that you can say!" Teresa exclaimed. "Sarah is in child services because of you!"

"Look, I'm sorry about all of this, I really am," Peter started. "But, I had a life before I met ya'll. This is what I do, ya know?"

"No, I didn't know," Isabel said. "And if I did, I wouldn't have been associating with you."

"You don't know how hard it is out here," Peter said.

"Never mind the fact that you are a drug dealer," Teresa said. "You took my youngest sister with you to deal!"

"I didn't know what else to do," Peter said.

"Well, you're out now," Teresa said. "You'll have time to figure it out."

Teresa and Isabel walked away. Peter stood there. He wanted to cry. But the tears just wouldn't pop out. So he just stood there not even wanting to be with himself. He just about didn't know who he was anymore.

Peter just decided to walk the streets. He needed time to think about what had gone down. He still couldn't believe that he put that family through all that. And he had lost something that had meant a lot to him. He felt as though he had found a new group of people to associate with. A new family. But that was not to be the case.

Peter wanted to drown his sorrows. He went to a bar nearby. He started drinking his favorite self-pity drink,

Scotch on the rocks. He kept on sipping, sipping, and sipping. He took Scotch pretty well, by glass five you wouldn't have noticed just how drunk he really was.

A beautiful woman named Selena walked in. She had on this sexy red dress and dirty blonde hair. Peter noticed her instantly just like everyone else in the bar. Peter saw her as an opportunity to drown his sorrows out the right way.

"Hey," Peter said.

"Hey," Selena replied.

"Are you lost?" Peter asked.

"Why would I be lost?" Selena replied.

"Usually, the only types of girls that look like you and walk in here are hookers," Peter explained.

"Well, I guess I am a first," Selena said.

Peter offered to buy Selena a drink. But Selena actually bought him a drink instead. And it was on from there. Both shared laughs and they shared stories. Selena was much more complicated than meets the eye. That was a rare thing for a woman that was as beautiful as her. She worked in marketing. But her dream was to become a fashion designer. She moved to Inglewood to save some money.

At this point, Peter was so drunk that he didn't care about anything as far as his actions were concerned. He took Selena outside and began to have sex with her on top of a car. She was drunk but she was so impressed with how he did not care that she allowed it. She even appeared that she was enjoying it.

The guy who owned the car walked out and he was clearly not impressed with Peter and Selena having sex on his car. He was downright disgusted with the sight. He looked like he was about to erupt. "What in Sam Hill?" The guy yelled.

"Who the fuck is Sam Hill?" Peter asked.

"What do you think you're doing?" The guy asked.

"Having sex," Peter answered. "I can tell you what you are doing. You are ruining the moment."

"Fuck you!" The guy barked.

That didn't deter Peter one bit. He continued to have sex with Selena while the guy stood there in shock. He decided to throw a beer can at Peter. Of course, this was a bad idea. Peter was a drug dealer from the hood. He was drunk and he didn't care. He got off of the car and gave the guy a menacing look. He then composed himself a second. It looked as though he had thought better of it. But that was not the case. He gave the guy a good one right in the face. The guy fell right down to the ground and was knocked out. Selena watched in half horror and half amazement.

Peter was shaking his hand. "Fuck!" he let out.

"That was amazing!" Selena said.

"I have to fucking get out of here!" Peter exclaimed.

Peter ran and called an Uber. He knew exactly what he had to do. He couldn't believe what he had lost due to his actions. He wanted to be with Teresa, Isabel, and Sarah. They had become his family. And he had let that go. He couldn't let that go. He had to do something. And fast.

The Uber stopped right in front of the apartment complex. He ran like he was in a Tom Hanks romantic comedy. He was ready to set things right. The only issue was that he was drunk too.

He stopped right in front of the door and began to ring the doorbell. He rang it repeatedly and just wouldn't stop. Then Teresa and Isabel came to door.

"Peter, what the hell are you doing?" Teresa asked with great annoyance.

"I'm sorry!" Peter yelled as he went to the ground.

"Peter, are you okay?" Isabel asked with concern.

"Yeah, I'm drunk," Peter said.

"You come to our door in the middle of the night, drunk?" Teresa asked in disbelief.

"It's because I can't let this go," Peter said. "I can't let this go through the cracks."

"You talk weird when you are drunk," Isabel commented.

"I didn't mean to get Sarah in trouble," Peter told them. "I just am in a tight spot, ya know?"

"Being a drug dealer is a tight spot, huh?" Teresa asked with disbelief.

"You know how it is!" Peter said. "It's tough out here! I've gotta make that bread. I have no other skills!"

Teresa and Isabel looked at Peter. They began to feel bad for him. It was clear that he just made a mistake. And that he just needed another chance. And he was ready to receive that said second chance.

They invited Peter in for some coffee and pancakes to sober him up. For a second, in Peter's drunken mind, he thought that he would be having a threesome with Teresa and Isabel. But he then realized how that was just not going to happen. That he should be just happy that he was here.

They brought up a nice stack with a cup of coffee. He couldn't hold back the smile on his face. For the first time in a long time, he felt as if he was actually somewhere that he belonged. He hadn't had that feeling in a long time, if ever. Things just felt so right.

"You guys are like my new family," Peter said.

"You are a sweet drunk," Teresa told Peter.

"Fuck!" Peter said causing Teresa and Isabel to laugh.

The three began to talk and laugh again. Teresa and Isabel remembered what made Peter a good guy. He may have been a drug dealer. But if anything, he was a drug dealer with a heart of gold. He meant well. And like he said, they were his new family. And they welcomed him in with open arms.

The next morning, Teresa and Isabel had to get to work. But they had no one to babysit Sarah. They had assumed that Peter would be hung over and in no shape to take care of her. But the doorbell began to ring. Teresa opened the door and it was better. He had bagels in his hand.

"Morning," Peter said with a big grin.

"Peter," Teresa said with surprise. "How are you awake?"

"I don't get hang overs," Peter said. "Need a babysitter?"

"Peter!" Sarah yelled as she ran to him. She gave him a nice tight hug.

"You sure?" Isabel asked.

"I don't think that I've been surer of anything," Peter said.

Teresa and Isabel smiled to each other. They weren't sure about things for a second there. But they knew that ultimately that they were in good hands and that's all that mattered.

That's What I'm Talking About

He watched the cheerleaders cheer while on the sidelines. They were actually practicing. But it was all the same to Josh Hamilton, the backup quarterback for the UCLA football team. Being a backup was cool in its own way. He was on the team. He got his own uniform. He got to party.

But he wasn't the starter. The starters get all the attention. The starters are the only ones that people care about. People actually knew their name. No one knew Josh's name. They could get with the cheerleaders. Maybe even two or three.

The starting quarterback was Todd Marks. Todd was a star on his high school football team in Texas. He was destined to become the next Drew Brees. He had the arm. He had the look. He was someone that everyone wanted to be around. Probably to ride off of his coat tails. But still, he had that *it* factor.

Josh always looked at Todd with admiration. Josh wished that he had *it*. If he just had *it* then maybe things would get better.

It wasn't as though life sucked for Josh. He could date here and there. People liked him overall. But Todd was with a new girl every night. Every girl wanted to be with him and every guy wanted to be him. And that was the difference between being the starting quarterback and the backup quarterback. Fame.

"All right, boys!" Coach Rids yelled. "Let's get down to business."

Everyone ran across the field to Coach Rids. Rids dreamed of coaching in the NFL. He had gotten that dream too. Years ago, he coached the Carolina Panthers. But for two seasons, they were dismal and he was quickly replaced. He was fortunate and got a multi-million dollar deal with UCLA. So, he wasn't hurting. But he really wanted to get back into the NFL. It's been five years since he was in the NFL fulltime. Three since he coached an NFL game period.

This gave Coach Rids a certain type of gravitas. Everyone respected him and looked up to him. He had coached in the NFL. Of course, he deserved all of the praise.

The work outs were as rigorous as you'd imagine. Probably more. He didn't care if you were a backup or not. You worked and you worked hard. Backups were more than likely upset over this. Nine times out of ten, they would never get on the grid iron unless there was a big blow out on their part or a surprise injury. It was good exercise though.

"I am fucking tired of this!" said Jalen, a backup tight end.

"We do all of this for nothing," said Tate, a backup running back.

"You never know guys," Josh said. "Shit happens."

"You sound like my mother," Jalen quipped. Everyone got a good laugh out of that.

It's true. Everyone's mothers would say things like this. It didn't matter though. The chances of getting on the field were slim to none. They just had to be ready on the off chance of something happening. Be prepared to take over in the face of a major disaster. Like a machine.

But it didn't make anyone feel better. In fact, it would make you feel worse. It became just another reminder of where they were at. They were just backups. The unsharpened pencils that were in the box. They had to sit back and watch the sharp pencils write away.

Going to parties was a fun thing though whether you were a starter or not. The girls at the school did not watch any games at all. They would only go to games so they could look cute in the gear. Or if they had boyfriends, they went because of their boyfriends dragging them to the games.

So going to these parties with any sign of being on the team was an aphrodisiac, if you will. Once a girl spotted that uniform they spotted potential. And that potential meant some kind of opportunity. And that opportunity could spell a lot of different things including, but not limited to, money.

Josh actually didn't like to party much. He felt that there was an air of fakeness in the air whenever he went to one of these. But Jalen and Tate dragged him here. They felt that it would be good for him.

"I just don't get this," Josh said as he looked around with some distress. "What is the point?"

"The point is that there is no point," Tate informed Josh.

"So, why do something pointless?" Josh asked.

"To unwind," Jalen said. "To forget about all of the bullshit."

A few very hot girls started walking by. Josh, Jalen, and Tate started to stare and their jaws were about to drop like the wolves in those old Warner Brothers cartoons. Those types of girls were a dime a dozen at these types of parties. Now, Josh could see how these parties could be fun.

Josh began to explore the party a bit. There were different kinds of actives that were taking place. There was a beer pong game taking place. One guy was brutally beating this other guy. Another guy was becoming so drunk that he couldn't even stand up straight. But he kept on smiling. So that was all that mattered.

Josh continued on. He saw this girl that was in the corner. She was different from the rest. Definitely hot. But different. She had super jet black hair. Very pale skin. Black eyes. And a black dress. She had this gothic thing going on without even trying. It all looked so natural. And he was intrigued. So, he walked over to her without much if any haste.

"You looking for something?" Josh asked.

"What do you mean?" the girl said.

"It looks like you are looking for something," Josh continued. "I just want to say that you don't need to look for anything. You have it all."

She looked at Josh in an interesting way after that. No one had ever said such lines to her. She became intrigued herself.

"Lori." She introduced herself extending her hand for a handshake.

"Josh," he said taking Lori's hand and kissing it. She nearly blushed.

"Well Josh, what brings you here?" Lori asked.

"My team," Josh told her.

"You are on the football team?" Lori asked very surprised.

"Yup," Josh said without skipping a beat.

"I would have never pegged you for a football player," Lori commented.

"Why?" Josh asked sincerely wondering the answer.

"Because usually they don't seem intelligent," Lori said.

Just as she said this, Tad was running around in a toga with a funnel of beer in his mouth. He had some other starters behind him running and yelling with him. It was a belligerent parade. Lori nodded to this to point out exactly what she meant by her comments.

"Most are," Josh said causing Lori to laugh.

"What position are you?" Lori asked trying to become interested in football. It was hard for her.

"Backup quarterback to the toga bro," Josh said.

"Ah, nice," Lori said. "Why did you get into football?"

"I am a masochist," Josh said causing Lori to laugh once again.

"I suppose that it's the perfect sport for that," Lori commented.

"You supposed right," Josh said.

Josh and Lori smiled at each with true warmth. A real connection was being built. Something that neither would have expected to happen coming to this party. They continued to talk for a very long time. They spoke about art, war, and technology. Josh discovered that Lori was a fashion major. She showed him her fashion designs and he was impressed with just how developed they were.

Lori discovered a few things about Josh as well. Josh was an anthropology major. He just liked primates. He figured that he'd have a career working in that field after college. He didn't think that he would have any chance at the NFL. Maybe the CFL or the IFL. But the NFL was reserved for starters like Tad.

Hours went by as the two continued to talk. The rest of the party didn't matter to them. Not that it did at the start. But they were so engaged with each other about what was taking place. Before they knew it, it was 3 am.

"It's getting late," Lori said.

"Night cap?" Josh said.

"Nice try," Lori said with a smile. "But we should see each other again." Lori took out a very slick ink pen and wrote her number on his hand. It wasn't just in the normal boring way. But the way that she was so cool and slick that just the writing turned Josh on.

"Great," Josh said trying to hide his enthusiasm. "I'll give you a call."

"Looking forward to it," Lori said.

The two went in for a hug. But Josh was feeling extra confident right now. The amount of alcohol that he had consumed had a little to do with this. He went and kissed Lori to her surprised. She didn't back out. She stayed in it and then he backed out. He was feeling pretty damn good.

"Thank you," Lori said quietly while blushing. She then walked away.

Josh decided that it was time that he go back to his dorm as well. He thought for sure that he'd be in bed by now. He didn't expect to be with a girl like Lori. He wasn't really into the type of girls that college had to offer. But she did not fit that bill. She set herself on another level.

As Josh walked out, he noticed Tad was lying on the ground with a lot of people around him. He went over to see what was going on. Tad was still in his toga and it appeared that he had broken his right leg. He also appeared to be in immense pain.

"What happened?" Josh asked.

"Tad was drunk so he decided to act like one of those guys from *Jackass*," answered Cliff, the starting wide receiver.

"Ah," Josh said trying to hide how he felt about the situation.

"Bro," Tad said talking to Josh.

"Are you okay, Tad?" Josh said.

"Bro, you are going to need to play," Tad said.

"What?" Josh asked.

"You are going to need to start," Tad explained. "This is all you." As he said this, the ambulance came and picked him up. Tad was instantly hauled off as everyone looked on. It was still sinking in what Tad had just informed Josh. He would indeed become the starter on the team. His life was about to change.

The next morning, Josh got a call from Coach Rids. He wanted to see him as soon as possible. Of course, Josh knew exactly what this was all about. He was pretty nervous at this point. He hadn't counted on anything like this happening. No one did. And usually things like this didn't happen. If Tad wasn't such an idiot then it would not have happened. But alas he was all of a sudden in this daunting position.

When Josh arrived to Coach Rids office, the offensive coordinator, Coach Dan, was there as well. They both had these very stern looks on their faces. For good reason. Their star quarterback was taken out.

"Hi Josh," Coach Rids said solemnly. "Come in."

Josh came inside and shut the door. They both begin to scan him almost immediately. They hadn't paid too much attention to him before being that he was a backup. But now that he was starting, they had to give him a more in depth look.

"Are you aware of what took place last night?" Coach Rids asked.

"Yes sir," Josh replied.

"This is one of the biggest hits that this team has taken in years," Coach Rids said making Josh even more nervous. "Tad's special, ya know?"

"I am aware, Sir," Josh said.

"But this is about you now," Coach Rids continued. "We need you to take this team by the reigns. Can you be tuned in, tapped on, and turned on? Can you lead us to glory?"

Josh felt that the way that Coach Rids went about things lacked a little bit. He was the backup quarterback. The second string quarterback. It was his job to be ready to go at a moment's notice. He didn't need any of the other mumbo jumbo bullshit that the coach was saying. But he understood why he was saying all of this. He was, in his own way, attempting to be inspirational. He was just doing a very poor job of it.

"I'm ready, Sir," Josh said.

"Excellent," Coach Rids said. "Now, Coach Dan and I will be there every step of the way."

Coach Dan turned to Josh in an awkward way. You could tell that he was still coming to terms with Tad's injury. He knew Josh well enough. But he loved Tad. He knew that with Tad great things would happen. He wanted to get to the NFL. So, he felt that Tad would be his ticket to the NFL. With Josh, it appeared as though he had gotten some consolation prize.

"Josh," Coach Dan started. "This team is going to need someone to band around. It's going to need a leader on this field. We are expecting you to become that leader. I know that you were a good quarterback at your high school. But this is a different field. A different arena. This is a quick game. And I know that you can handle this."

This gave Josh some chills. Coach Dan got right to his bones. This was going to be a huge uphill battle for him. He was planning on sitting on the bench and watching Tad do his thing. Now, he was going to be Tad. Only, he was not as good as Tad. He was going to have to step up.

Coach Rids dismissed Josh to practice. He'd been practicing since the summer. But this was different. He was going to practice as the starting quarterback going into the first game of the season. He could feel the butterflies flying inside of his stomach. And then he could feel the butterflies punching the wall of his stomach. Nerve wrecking wouldn't even begin to cover it.

Josh was now practicing with a whole new group; the starters: Cliff, the wide receiver; Johnny, the tight end; Davey, the running back and a host of others. They all looked at Josh in a weird way. They knew him. They'd seen him practice. But Tad was their boy. And they trusted him. Of course, they had no idea how much they could trust Josh.

Josh figured that he had to start to set the tone for the entire team. He had to start things off on the right note. He remembered when he started really getting into this in high school and how it affected his team. They were barely removed from high school; it would have to be the same deal.

Josh got in the middle of the whole team. Everyone was staring at him not exactly sure what he was doing. Josh, himself, didn't know exactly what he was doing. But he knew that it would have impact. And he was in desperate need of that.

"Hey guys," Josh said. "Clearly, we're going through a tough time. Tad is a great guy and a great quarterback. This is his team. But I am going to do my damnest to make sure that he has the best team available when he is ready to return. We are going to go out there with the mentality of business as usual."

It really wasn't much. But it was something. And that something was just enough of a push for everyone. No one had expected for Josh to just come up like that in front of everyone and begin to speak in such a manner. That was impressive enough to them to ignite some inspiration. Everyone began to clap and cheer. It began with a slow clap and then everyone went wild. Josh stood there, a bit surprised, and a bit pleased with himself. The speech wasn't even that good to him. But that wasn't the point. He went out and made an effort. And this was just what would ignite the team's spirits.

Everyone practiced harder than ever before. It was as if everyone had a shot of adrenaline pumped into them. They were playing for Tad, of course. But they were playing for Josh. They hadn't expected any kind of leadership from Josh at all. And they had just gotten what they had needed.

Josh had instant chemistry with Cliff, Johnny, and Davey. It felt as though they were continuing something that they had started once before. It was nearly effortless. And as they continued to play with each other, the confidence between the four of them only grew.

Coach Rids and Coach Dan watched practice in amazement. They had hoped for the best. But realistically, they had expected the worst. Instead, they got a team that united together under excruciating circumstances. It gave them this warm feeling in their hearts that they both instantly attempted to hide from each other.

The practice was a session. The chemistry that Josh had with the rest of the starters was looking good. The starters really started to like Josh. They didn't realize how cool he was. And how smart he was. Not that Tad wasn't smart. Indeed, he was. But he was smart about football. And seemingly nothing else. Josh could talk about anything.

"Josh man, we're going to party tonight," Davey said. "You gotta come."

"Yeah bro," Johnny said. "It's going be lit."

"Sure," Josh said with something clearly on his mind. "But I have to make a call."

Josh went to the side and looked into his phone. He stared at Lori's phone number. In the back of his head, he had been thinking about her all day. She was just so different than another other girls that he had ever met. And he was excited to really get to know her.

He didn't hesitate and dialed her number. He was ready to talk her. The great practice session had filled him with zest and confidence that he had never experienced before. He had some swagger now.

"Hello?" Lori said.

"Hey, it's Josh," he said with some real swagger.

"Oh hey!" Lori said excited. "I was wondering when you would call."

"I was at practice," Josh explained. "There was a big issue today."

"What happened?" Lori asked with genuine concern. She had no idea of what had taken place.

"Tad, the starter, broke his leg at the party that we were at last night," Josh explained. "So now, I am the interim starter."

"Oh shit!" Lori exclaimed. "I'm sorry about that. Must be tough."

"It is," Josh said. "But today went great. I'm looking forward to the game."

"Well, that's good," Lori said.

"There's this party that I got invited to by the guys," Josh said. "You should come with me."

"I thought that we weren't party people?" Lori asked a bit confused.

"Yeah, but I figured that this would be a good team bonding experience," Josh explained.

Lori was a bit thrown off by this. It wasn't that Josh had changed overnight. But she didn't expect to be invited to some party. She thought that they would do something cool and off beat like go to some alternative art show. But at the same time, his team did invite him, so it would be a good thing to go.

"I'd love to go," Lori said.

"Sweet!" Josh exclaimed, not being able to hold in his excitement. "Let's meet up around the library at nine."

"Sounds good," Lori said.

"See you then," Josh said.

"See you then," Lori said.

Josh ended the call and turned to the guys. He gave them indication that he was in and they all rallied around him. He couldn't believe what was happening. He felt bad for Tad and all. But this was just so good to him. To have the whole team liking him and looking up to him just felt so good.

Later that night, Josh met Lori at the library. When they saw each other, it was like two star crossed lovers had just reunited. But Lori could sense just a smidgen of a difference in Josh. Not that it was bad. But he wasn't 100% the same guy that she had just met.

"Hey, hey!" Josh said as he embraced Lori.

"Hey there," Lori said.

The two began walking to the party. The conversation between the two was not what Lori expected. Josh was going on about how well the practice session went. It wasn't that Lori didn't care. But she didn't think that Josh would care as much. He was so excited about it. She would start talking about something else. And he would join her in that. But he seemed to be able to direct the conversation back to football.

Once they arrived at the party, Josh seemed to have gone to another level. Cliff came out and warmly greeted Josh. He handed Josh a beer and challenged him to shotgun the beer. Josh in turn challenged him to shotgun his beer. They both ended up doing this. Josh won by a nose. Lori watched with slight horror.

They went inside and Josh continued to get drunk. The drunker he got, the more he seemed to adopt a bro like mentality. And by bro like mentality that meant that he had regressed from the interesting, cool, off beat guy to some frat boy. And Lori did not like frat boys.

"Wanna try?" Josh said as he pushed his margarita to Lori's face.

"No, I'm good," Lori replied. "What's going on?"

"What do you mean what's going on?" Josh asked.

"Why are you acting this way?" Lori put it bluntly.

"I'm just trying to have fun!" Josh stated. "Lighten up!"

It was true; he was just trying to have fun. Lori couldn't blame him for that. The thing is that this wasn't what attracted Lori to him. What attracted her to him was who he was last night. She liked him because he was different. But with his current state of being, he was no different than most guys.

"Don't you think that you are conforming just a bit?" Lori asked. "I mean, just a bit?"

"No," Josh replied. "Not really. Why do you say that?"

"Because in one night you've changed," Lori said.

"How?" Josh asked.

"Just observe your behavior," Lori said.

"Look," Josh started. "You do not even know me. You have no right to say any of this."

Lori was taken aback by Josh. He was acting like some kind of a douche. Most women, whether they would like to admit or not, liked douches. But not Lori. She had enough of them in high. And Josh was starting to show himself to be a bit of a douche.

Davey brought in a funnel with a keg attached. He charged in right to Josh. He challenged him to drink from the funnel. Josh accepted this challenge. He began to drink like a champion. It impressed everyone around him just how much beer that he could consume. Everyone except for Lori that is. She had just about had it.

"Who are you?" Lori asked with some anger behind her words.

"What is your deal?" Josh asked super drunk. "Fucking relax."

"I wanted to go with you, not some frat boy asshole," Lori said.

"I'm just partying," Josh said. "Don't you like to party?"

"Not really," Lori told him. "And I thought that you didn't."

"People change," Josh said.

"I guess you are right about that," Lori said. And with that she walked away. At first, Josh tried to stop her. But she wasn't having it. She didn't like where Josh was heading. And she didn't want to find out where he was going to land.

Josh watched her walk away. He began to get upset. He really liked Lori. He really wanted to be with her. And being as drunk as he was at the moment, he really wanted to have sex with her. But he had blown it. He wasn't 100% sure how he did. But he knew that he did something wrong.

Josh had to drown his sorrows. So he decided to go in and drink more. He just drank, drank, and drank. He didn't even eat some chips to level himself out. He just drank and got drunker. The fact that he didn't vomit was a testament to his stomach of steel. Everyone watched him in amazement as though he was still on the grid iron practicing.

The next morning, Josh woke up in his bed. Now, this would be fine and dandy. But he had no idea on how he made it to his bed. Josh had realized that he had blacked out. It made sense considering just what he had consumed. He didn't have much of a hangover, if any. He considered himself lucky.

He realized that he was late for practice. He took a quick shower, got his gear and ran as fast as he could. He just jetted to practice. His second day as the starter and he was already late. The shame of the previous night was starting to set in.

When he got there Coach Rids and Coach Dan were waiting for him. Josh could tell by their body language that they were not very happy with him being late. The rest of the team was already on the field.

"Josh," Coach Dan said. "Chat time."

Coach Dan took Josh aside. Josh feared the worst. Maybe the third string quarterback was about to get the nod due to Josh's behavior. He could totally see that happening. And he would have deserved it. One good practice had completely gone to his head. He hadn't even played a game yet and he was acting like a rock star. The worst part about it was that he was on the slow road to that.

"Josh," Coach Dan started. "Don't be influenced. Be an influencer."

"Can you elaborate?" Josh asked.

"My guess is that you had a bit of a wild night," Coach Dan said.

Josh nodded.

"It's okay to have fun. Life needed some spice to it. But don't let it get to your head. Don't let these guys get you off track. Yes, you need to be here for the team. But you need to be here for yourself. You also need to be yourself. Don't change because your position has changed. That is the true test of a man."

Josh stood there in awe of Coach Dan's words. He began to think about how it related to him. He couldn't believe how much he had changed in such a short period of time. He had become someone that he would have previously thought was bullshit. And it ruined what could have been a relationship with Lori. He hadn't felt so embarrassed in such a long time.

Coach Dan dismissed him to the field. Josh decided from that point on that he was going to act a certain way. He put his blinders on and began to practice. And he had an even better practice than before. It wasn't just because he wanted the team to do well. He wanted himself to do well. It appeared than something more had gotten into him. A greater sense of self had gotten into him.

After practice, Josh rushed to find Lori. The team tried to convince him to hang out and grab a bite to eat. But he had no time for that. He knew what he had to do. He had to right the ship with Lori. He couldn't believe just how far off course that he had gotten with her.

He had no idea where she would be. But then an idea came to his head. And then he knew exactly where she would be. It became so beautifully obvious to him just where she would be at this very moment.

He went over to the fashion department. He saw Lori there putting the finishing touches on a dress that she had created. It was an interesting dress to say the least. It had this weird Gothic feel to it. It looked like something that Tim Burton would have designed if he worked for some big time fashion company.

"Lori!" Josh shouted out. Lori turned and got goose bumps instantly.

"Yeah?" Lori said, trying to keep her cool.

"Chat time," Josh said stealing that same line from Coach Dan.

"No time," Lori said as she continued to work on her dress.

"It looks like you need a model," Josh commented.

"I do," Lori said.

"Well..." Josh started. "I'm here."

Lori looked at Josh with major intrigue. He wanted to make things right so badly that he was willing to model her dress. She made sure to hide how this made her feel to come off more cool and indifferent. "Well..." Lori started. "Hop to it."

Josh went in and started to get into the dress. Lori really enjoyed fitting him in it. She made sure to take her time sliding him into the dress. He was going to have to savor every moment of this whether he liked it or not. She made sure that he looked as pretty as possible.

"Lori," Josh started. "Yesterday was the weirdest day of my life. I went from a backup quarterback to a starting quarterback on a division one college football team. It was a major head fuck. And to top it off, I was killing it. I know it's no excuse. But I started going down the wrong road. I'm sorry."

Lori was listening the whole time. She didn't know what to say. He sounded sincere and he was doing this for her. He clearly cared about her. Perhaps, it would be okay to let him off the hook.

Josh stood there in all of the glory of the dress. Lori looked at him and couldn't help smiling. She was impressed with his commitment. She had never meant a guy that was willing to go to these kinds of lengths.

"How do I look?" Josh asked.

"Like a drag queen," Lori said.

"As long as I am pretty," Josh commented making Lori laugh.

"What are you?" Lori said with a smile.

"The coolest, uncool guy ever," Josh said.

Josh then leaned in and kissed Lori. One thing that has stuck with him was his confidence level being on the rise. He knew that at the end of the day that as long as he could look in the mirror and know who he was that he was on the right path. No matter how cheesy that felt or sounded. That revelation worked, he won Lori back.

Some people walked by and were caught off guard seeing Lori and what looked like a girl kissing. They didn't know exactly what to make of it. But it was Los Angeles; they were used to things like this already.

"I usually save making dinner for the third date," Josh told Lori.

"I suppose that works," Lori said.

"Ya know what?" Josh said. "I think that I could get used to this outfit."

"Oh no," Lori said. "My boyfriend won't be wearing a dress."

"Boyfriend?" Josh said with a sly smile.

"I mean," Lori said a little shy after being caught.

Josh looked Lori right in the eyes and gave her another big kiss. It didn't matter that more people came in and began to stare at them wondering just what the hell was going on. Though Josh did realize that they were creating a scene. "Let's get out of here," he requested.

And they went to Josh's dorm. He cooked her some pasta. He made some amazing meat sauce. When Lori asked him where he got the recipe from, he told her that it was actually his mother's recipe. But of course, he didn't make it as good as his mom. This made Lori like him even more. Gone was the bro like behavior. This was the real Josh Hamilton. And she dug it.

After a nice dinner, Josh put on a movie. It was *Beetlejuice*. He knew exactly what he was doing. If he had put on some movie like *The Notebook*, it would have been too obvious. But *Beetlejuice*? His intentions weren't 100% clear. Just clear enough.

It wasn't too long before they began to ignore what was going on the screen and were solely focused on each other. Things began to escalate and then they began to have sex. It was more than what Josh had imagined. It was just about as mystical as something could be in real life. They went at it all night and slept in each other's arms.

The next morning Josh awoke with Lori in his arms. It was game day as well. But he wasn't nervous. All was right with the world. And he knew where he belonged. His hero's welcome was right in her arms.

Come to My Window

Summer was always just a weird time to me. I loved it of course. Who didn't want to not be in school? And the weather was amazing. I could sleep in all day. I was only 12 so I didn't have to work. Things felt so good.

The only thing that sucked was the simple fact that I had no friends. I really had nowhere to go. The only thing that I did during summer vacation was go away on vacation for a week or two. We were going to Walt Disney World so I was very much looking forward to that.

While the people in my school hung out with each other, I was left to be by myself. I wasn't really lonely per say. I didn't really want to hang out with the guys at the school. And while there were some girls that I did find attractive, I didn't really want to hang out with them either. There was something about these girls that just wasn't very cool. They were nice one moment, and then mean the next. Maybe it was just hormones. Usually, those girls went for guys who treated them like dirt. I enjoyed being a nice guy for the most part.

So while my peers were hanging out with each other and convincing themselves that they were having "fun", I had other ideas. I decided to dive into different pursuits. One of which was teaching myself the most effective ways

But then, to my surprise, a girl with a helmet popped out. She had raven hair, she wore glasses, and her face looked nice and soft. I couldn't believe it. It was a female driver. She could be the next Danica Patrick for all I knew.

I knew that had to go up to talk to her. Then all of the resistance in my body started to build. I've kissed a girl before, and I had just had my first girlfriend. But that did not end well. She actually dumped me without telling me. Needless to say that was very awkward for the both of us. But especially me.

The fear of something like that happening was apparent. Instead of the force being with me, the nerves were with me. But alas, I was freaking out over conjecture. Who's to say that she would even be into me? It would behoove me to go up and see what she said first. Then see what would take place.

I managed to get some courage in my body and get myself to walk over and talk to her. I had to calm my mind down. I had one shot here. I did not want to ruin it. I kept repeating the mantra ""don't fuck up" in my head.

I got right in front of her and she looked right me. She was more beautiful close up. And she wore zero make up. I wish that I went to school with a girl like this. They are were into the same old bullshit. It all probably surrounded make up and my little pony. Now there were bronies out there. And I liked the powerpuff girls just as much as the next guy. But there had to be more depth to girls' right?

"Hi," I mustered out.

"Hi," she said.

"I'm Todd," I introduced myself.

"Monica," she said.

"You're a race car driver?" I asked trying to make myself not shake.

"And you can only talk in one sentence," Monica said glad he seemed to have a sense of humor.

"Yeah, that's a special talent of mine," I said making Monica giggle a little bit. "It's taken a while, but I've honed it."

"Everything takes time I suppose," Monica said. "But yeah, I race. Do you?"

"I wish," I said. "I want to, but I guess I am too financially challenged. I stick to go karts." Monica started laughing again. I was slowly, but surely winning her over. Nice.

"Maybe one day you'll overcome it," Monica said.

"How come I've never seen you here?" I asked.

"I've been racing at Hagerstown," Monica answered. 'They are off his weekend. So I thought that I'd give Potomac a go."

"I think you'll dig it," I told her. "Just don't eat the hot dogs."

"Why do you say that?" she asked with legitimate concern.

"They're red," I informed her. "Hot dogs aren't supposed to be red."

She couldn't help but crack up over this. We continued to talk about anything and everything. She lived about thirty minutes away from me. She started racing when she was eight in go karts. She ran mini stocks and just moved up to hobby stocks. She was 13 years old so that was bonus. She won a bunch of go kart races. She hadn't managed to win in mini stocks. But she came rather close. She was easily the coolest chick that have ever met before. My luck had finally came in. She was the unicorn that I've been looking for all my life. The lyrics "all my life, I've prayed for someone like you. And I thank God that I've finally found you. For all my life, I've prayed for someone like you. "And I know that you feel the same way too." Were playing in my head. I could have breaked into a happy dance.

Before we knew it, it was time for the drivers meeting. It wasn't like NASCAR where the drivers meeting was in some nice building. It was just outside the food stand in the garage.

A man named Pete Horace ran the drivers meeting. He was essentially our commissioner. He had been around for a minute. His hair was whiter than Steve Martin's. He did love racing though. It was more than crystal clear that it was his life purpose. And he spoke with every fiber of his being at these meetings.

Pete was very matter of fact. He explained the rules the same way every week. There would be updates here and there. If anyone did something stupid the previous race he would make sure to call them out. But nine times out of ten it was usually the same thing. And no one would have it any other way.

As luck would have had it, the hobby stocks were the first ones out. They had their hot laps, heat race, and then their A main. I was beyond stoke to see Monica race. I wanted to see how she stacked up against the drivers down here at Potomac. Potomac had some pretty good drivers. There was this one guy who ran at the motor cross on the same property. And he was a good driver. His older brother ran at the motorscross track as well and killed it in Hobby Stocks before getting the car to dirt late models. The point was that it was a tough series. It would interesting to see how she stacked up.

I next to her car as she climbed in and got herself ready. He father came by. He looked at me with suspicion at first. Any father does that when a guy dares to venture near their little girl.

"Can I help you son?' he asked trying to scare me.

"Hey, I'm Todd," I said, trying to be intimidated.

"Dad, he's cool," Monica told him.

Her dad began to look me over. He surveyed me to see if I was going to be any kind of threat. Perhaps he felt that I was going to be a distraction to her or something. But Monica wasn't having of his behavior. So he simply walked away. It appeared as though I was going to be in the clear.

"So," I started. "How do you think you are going to do?"

"I don't know," she answered honestly. "I've gotta learn the track first. Then we'll go from there."

"Good answer," I told her.

"I thought as much," she said.

I could tell that she was getting into the zone. So I began to back away to allow her to clear her head a bit. She had never even been to this track before. So I could only imagine how nervous she would be.

I got to the infield with Clark. He was hanging out with one of the officials. Clark looked at me in a way that he had never looked at me before. I didn't quite get what was up with that. He wouldn't stop looking at me like this either.

"What's going on?" I asked Clark hoping that he'd clarify this for me.

"Seen you with the new Danica Patrick," Clark said.

"Ah," I said understanding what the looks were all about.

"She seems nice," Clark said. "She has squeezable tits."

"C'mon, Clark," I said. Clark enjoyed making comments like this.

"What?" Clark said, completely self-aware. It's not that he knew exactly what he said and stood by it. He didn't even realize how what he was wrong.

The hot laps began. Monica looked pretty decent. She got loose once. But she showed some decent speed. There were 22 cars in the field and she was about the 10th quickest car. That was pretty good.

"Well look at that," Mark commented. "She can hang."

She can hang indeed.

She went back to the garage and started working on her car. I wanted to give her space and watch the other hot laps. So I figured that I'd just catch up with her after her A main. Didn't want to crowd.

Before I knew it, it was time for her heat race. The heat race was only eight laps. She drew a second starting position. So the chances of her gaining a good starting spot for the A main was going. The top three in each heat race were locked into a top three starting positions. After that the field was basically put in a pinball to decide on where people would be starting.

The heat race was short and entertaining. Monica battled hard for the lead. I think that she was able to get a pretty good feel for the track based off of those hot laps. She just wasn't quite as good as the lead car, Barney Marks. This was Barney's third year in the series so, fair enough.

Monica held on to second for a while. But another veteran, Timothy Crafton, got by her on the last lap. So she finished third in her heat. She was going to start finish. Not bad, not bad.

I watched another heat race. But I was getting anxious. I was so excited for Monica. I wanted to see her again. I wanted to see what was in her head. And of course I wanted her to see me as an option. Could you imagine my second girlfriend being a race car driver?

Once the heat race for min stocks was over, I rushed over to her car in the garage. She stood there eating a hot dog. She had a diet coke in hand as well. This may have to do with the fact that most girls like to say that "I eat healthy" and not eat stuff like that. But she didn't seem to care about that. And she still had a rock solid body at that.

"I thought I warned you about that hot dog?" I said to her as I walked in.

"Had to take the leap," Monica said as she scarfed down the dog.

"What did you think of it being red?" I asked her.

"Red is fine with me," Monica replied. "Blue or yellow would be weird. Unless, it was Dr. Seuss's' birthday."

Look at her, she had smart jokes. No wonder I was so attracted to her. I know that I keep beating this horse. But if I will dammed she is cool. She was saying jokes that I would be saying and the made fun of after the fact.

"You going to win?" I asked, half-jokingly.

"Maybe if a few of these guys wreck," She said maybe a quarter of the way joking. "These guys are good."

"They've been running for a while," I informed her. "If they weren't good, I'd tell them to go back to go karts."

"Trueee," Monica said in a kind of goofy way. "Any advice for the race?"

"But I don't race," I told Monica.

"But you watch all these races," Monica said. "You should know the line."

She was right. Damn. She was absolutely right. I've watched so many races here. I knew the line just about as good as anyone. Another reason why I was falling for Monica. She empowered me.

"The high line always seems to come in," I told her. "I know that you are going to be starting on the bottom. But fight like hell to maintain fifth and get on the outside. If there's a restart and you restart on the outside, you can gain two spots out there if you can really get going."

"See," Monica said. "This is the stuff that I needed to know. You sir, are a pro."

"Well, ya know," I said. If I could have blushed, I would have.

Before we knew it, it was time for the Hobby stock race. I gave Monica a big hug. She gave me a kiss my cheek before going in her cockpit.

"See you after the race," She said as she climbed inside and buckled up.

I walked as she drove on the to track. She gave me a nice wave. Usually I just sunk myself into the racing when I went here. I hardly ever interacted with anyone outside of Clark when I was here. I may help out a team or two. But that was about. But this connecting thing was a little new to me. I didn't think that Potomac Speedway would be of that kind of interest to me. It seemed like I just learned something new today.

I got in just time before the race started. Clark was there waiting for me. He had that same look on his face that he had early on. It's like he had planted a camera on me. Maybe he did and I just didn't know.

"You going to wipe that look off of her face?" I asked him.

"You going to fuck her?" Clark asked bluntly.

"That's private," I told him. "And I am only 12."

"Never too early to get it in," Clark quipped.

The one to go was given on track. My anxiety level for Monica grew. I wanted to see her do well in the A main. It was only 20 laps. But a lot of crazy things can take place in 20 laps. And she could be the victim of that. It was weird wanting someone to do well outside of being a fan of them.

The green flag was flown. And it looked like Monica more than took my advice. She took it three wide and was in third. She slid up to the high side and nearly jumped the cushion. But she was able to stay in third. Everyone that was watching was impressed by this maneuver. If she was anything, she was aggressive. Yet there was a smoothness to her.

She ran hard. She raced around some of the best drivers of the series. They probably didn't even know who they were racing against. I cheered her on like a legit fan boy. It was really fun to see her slide through the dirt like that.

It was one of those nights though. The race was pretty insane. Cautions started to fly. It first started with those pesky single car spins. Then multiple cars began to pile up. Then one car, Nick Lowery, got loose under three other cars when they were in a four wide. Everyone cringed when they saw this. But, no one more than me.

Suddenly, Monica was put into the wall. Not extremely hard. But she had some serious damage because of it. There was a makeshift pit road at Potomac Speedway. She had to come down and get some helped.

I rushed down to her car and began to pull on her fenders. I think she saw me at the corner of her eye. I wasn't doing this to impress her. I felt bad that her good run was ruined because of some overzealous driver. It's a shame whenever that happens. But I suppose that's just racing.

The race finished up with a photo finish and that was just the first A main of the night. But for the first time ever I didn't really care about that A main. The only thing I cared about at the time was Monica. I might just be infatuated. But she did expect to see me after the race.

I went to her as she stood at the car with his dad. She was wiping the sweat off of her face. She looked very disappointed. But when she saw me her face lighten up a bit. I was glad that I could have that effect on her.

"Hey girl," I said, trying to sound like Ryan Gosling. "Great effort."

"Not so great finish," Monica quipped as she drank her Gatorade.

"That guy is an idiot," I told her.

"Certainly ran like one," Her dad said. Monica gave the signal to leave. He did gratefully.

"Until that point, it was fun to watch you," I told her.

"What can I say?" Monica said. "I try to put on a show each time out. Thanks for helping me out by the way."

"Oh," I said trying to sound bashful. "I didn't realize that you saw me."

"Of course I did," Monica said. "That was super cool of you."

Monica gave me a big hug. The type of hug that you give someone after a rough day. Then she did something that I didn't see coming. She kissed me right on the lips. It was nice and warm. A tad wet. But it felt very good.

"Call me," she said as she took my cell phone and put her number in my phone.

She then walked away to her dad to start preparing to load up and go home. I stood there for a second trying to piece what just happened. That was just amazing. In one day I went from all alone to a budding romance.